The Legend of Vanx Malic

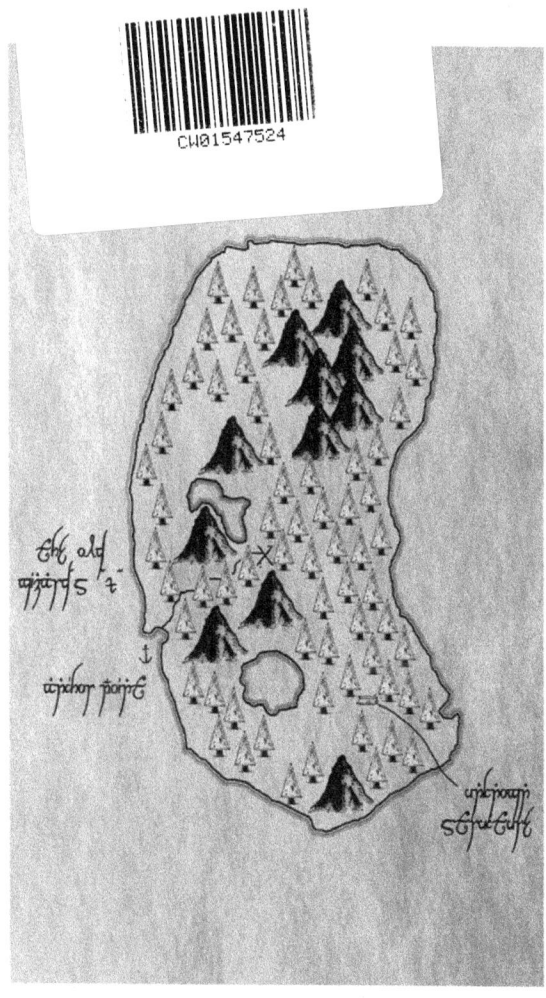

M. R. MATHIAS

Chapter One

Sometimes we must sacrifice a single branch for the good of a tree. For if we do not, we may lose many more, and even the tree itself. A Heart Tree is no exception.

- The Tome of Arbor

Vanx Malic reached the top of the hill they'd been climbing. Once he was at the treeless ridge, and could see both sides of the slope, he squatted down to scratch Sir Poopsalot, his canine familiar, behind the ears. He looked over the treetops at the lake below, and then up at the single great hawk circling high above. Even though summer was at its end, the tropical climate had the air thick with moisture and, already, his clothes were starting to stick to his skin.

Vanx had to shade the sun from his eyes just to see them up there. Papri, the elf, was on that bird's back and, though Vanx couldn't see them, he knew there were two other great hawks not far away. Papri was mapping the interior of the island from a literal bird's eye view. Vanx and the crew of his ship, *Adventurer*, had mapped the island's shoreline the last time they came here. He hoped the little guy took the time to estimate elevations and depressions in the terrain, and such.

Another glance down at the lake, and the path they would have to take through the foliage, made Vanx smile. The canopy was lush and green, but the trees were old, and the thick trunks allowed plenty of space between them. Papri was up there in the hot sun. Vanx, and those on foot with him, would be in the shade just as soon as they started down.

Like most things, Vanx wanted to do the mapping himself, but since his group was searching for a place to smash the ruby gem-seed, he left it to the least capable of the elves. When it came to elves, Papri wasn't the brightest ember in the firepit, but he followed Moonsy's orders without hesitation and wasn't afraid to do his share of the dirty work.

"There?" Chelda, a seven and a half foot tall, blonde gargan woman, pointed at a large boulder that was about two thirds of the way toward the fresh water. She was wearing light traveling garb and had a mountaineer's backpack slung on her wide shoulders. The tree tops were open there and a mote filled ray of sunlight shone on the spot as if the heavens concurred.

"Looks good to me." Vanx shrugged. His best friend Zeezle was back on Dragon Isle tending Chelda's horses and trying to get familiar with a dragon he'd been observing. Vanx wished the expert adventurer was here with them. Zeezle's insight would have been invaluable. Master Ruuk had returned to Zyth, so his ages old, wizardly intellect wouldn't be of use either.

"Your tree will have plenty of water," General Gloryvine Moonseed agreed. Moonsy, as they called her, was Chelda's lover, and an elf. She stood waist tall to her mate and had almost the same shade of blonde hair but, unlike Chelda, she was wearing her leather uniform, which included a finely crafted, chainmail shirt. Moonsy wasn't focused on the big rock. She looked back, past Vanx, down at the other of the three elves and the man she was conversing with. Vanx couldn't help but look, too. But his eyes drifted past them to the sea, and his single-masted ship anchored in the bay. Ronzon was on deck in a hammock, watching a fishing line.

Vanx was envious.

Anitha, the elf, and Castovanti, the sea mage, had fallen behind; Castovanti because he was an unfit human, and the exertion of the slightly graded climb they were making was getting to his lazy sea legs, Anitha because she was explaining some herb lore to

THE LEGEND OF VANX MALIC

Book Nine - The Tome of Arbor

M.R. Mathias

To hear about new releases, sales and giveaways,
follow M. R. Mathias @DahgMahn on Facebook,
Twitter, and Instagram, or visit www.mrmathias.com

All rights reserved. No part of this book may be reproduced,
scanned, or distributed in any form, including digital,
electronic, or mechanical, to include photocopying, recording,
or by any information storage and retrieval system, without
the prior written consent of the author, except for brief quotes
used in reviews.

This book is a work of fiction. All characters, names, places,
and incidents are products of the author's imagination or are
used fictitiously. Any resemblance to any actual persons, living
or dead, events or locales, is entirely coincidental.

ISBN: 978-1-946187-36-9
Mathias Publishing
2016 Condensed Pocket Paperback
Created in the United States of America
Worldwide Rights

M. R. MATHIAS

The Legend of Vanx Malic

This is for Mister Stubbs,
who never fails to come sit with me
when he hears the keyboard start clacking.

I would also like to thank,
Michael E. McPartland,
for creating "Papri's Map"

M. R. MATHIAS

the man. She kept his pace out of sympathy, Vanx was sure, for she could teleport herself up the hill, or run up it, as Gallarael had done.

Anitha was also in uniform. She keeping herself two steps ahead of Castovanti, just to stay eye to eye while they conversed.

"Look at that!" Chelda brought Vanx's attention back to the boulder. A sleek looking black feline creature, somewhat like a tailless panther, only with strange limb joints that didn't bend in a normal fashion, stood on the rock now.

"Gallarael must agree, too," Moonsy offered.

"Yah," Chelda added. "Is that the place, Vanx?"

"Yup, I guess it is." Vanx stood up and let the dog he was scratching start down ahead of him. "It would probably be best if everyone but me stayed on the backside of the ridge, about where Castovanti and Anitha are now."

"Yah," Chelda agreed, nodding at Moonsy. "All the chips and dust from the ruby will stick in your skin if you are near it. I've seen it." The gargan woman looked at Vanx, who was eye level to her now, but only because he was upslope. She was a head taller than he, and he knew exactly what she was about to ask.

"Who will sma—"

"You can do it, Chelda." Vanx smiled at her eagerness. Sometimes she acted like a great big, excited young girl. Other than Poops, as he called his dog, he'd known her longer than anyone with them. "But I'm going with you, Chel. Moonsy, I'll need the Glaive of Gladiolus, just in case we get that stuff on us."

The glaive was an ancient elven weapon created to heal the terrible creations the Hoar Witch used to torment the elves who lived under the Heart Tree near Saint Elm's Deep. It wasn't needed for defense from the old crone anymore because Vanx had captured her, and Pwca had killed her, but it still healed anyone it poked. After they smashed the ruby gem-seed on the rock, one or both of them would probably need to use that power.

Get Gallarael and return, Poops, Vanx used his mind to speak to the dog. Even though Vanx didn't like it all that much, he was a warlock of sorts, and a few other things as well. Poops wasn't just a pet, either. He was Vanx's wizardly familiar.

"Come on Chelda." Vanx started past the two love struck women, toward the boulder.

"I'll go back and stay the two laggers," Moonsy said, handing Vanx the blade, hilt first, as he passed. The Glaive of Gladiolus looked like a sword in Moonsy's hands, and like a fancy long dagger in his. When Chelda held it, it looked like a table knife.

Poops was coming back up, but Gallarael was nowhere to be seen. When she was in her changeling forms, it made Vanx uneasy, and she knew it. He wouldn't see her again until the deed was done, and then only when she decided to shift shapes back to her humanly self.

"We are not going to Harthgar, Chel." Vanx scoffed at the way his huge friend bent down and kissed Moonsy goodbye. "You'll be back up the hill in no time."

"Bye, love," Chelda whispered and started after Vanx. He only heard her words because he was sinking into Sir Poopsalot's senses again. The dog's keen perceptions were now Vanx's, too.

Vanx tried to ignore the strong smell of brine in the air and let the hill force his pace into a jog, but he was in no hurry. After they crushed the gem, which was some sort of magical Heart Tree seed, they still had to search the sizable island. Vanx's Goddess had told him that only after they broke the ruby open here, would he find out where the other three seed-gems were, and where he should take them to be released.

It was no small atoll they were on. Vanx knew that, besides the hungry, ship-sized crabs, and the red marked spiders that almost killed Zeezle, there was something else roaming this place, something that left paw prints deep enough to fill with water and bathe in. It was a big island. Far bigger than Vanx remembered. And if they had to go into the boreholes, like before, there was the deadly tentacled beast he never completely saw, and who knew what else.

Smashing the gem-seed was the first thing they had to do, and he was ready to get on with it.

"Let's get this part done," he said.

"Yah," Chelda agreed.

Chapter Two

> He took her to the river,
> and he swore his love was true.
> And then his Molly kissed him,
> and said I love *me* too.
> – Parydon Cobbles

After Vanx placed the ruby on the boulder, Chelda raised the warhammer Pyra had let them take from her hoard, high overhead, and paused there, looking at Vanx. He had an urge to make her stay poised that way for a while by ignoring her, but now wasn't the time for pranks.

Vanx gave her a nod and dropped to the ground. Chelda brought the heavy head-basher down so fast that he almost didn't get under the expanding ring of jewel dust that exploded outward when it hit.

At first, the sound of fleeing birds, cawing and flapping madly, was all that he could hear, but then the *whoosh* of the powerful stuff Chelda released took over and drowned out the world.

Chelda fell beside him, her blouse was tattered, and her whole upper torso was covered in jewel dust. Some of the particles were in her skin so deep that she had blood trailing down her cheeks like tears. There was a larger chip of ruby stuck in her neck, right behind her ear. Blood ran over her shoulder and right down into her ample cleavage.

Vanx had to shake his head when she grinned at him triumphantly. He stuck her with the Glaive of Gladiolus, and then poked the tip of the sword into his forearm, just in case. In a matter of seconds, the foreign matter was forced from Chelda's skin, and the cuts and slices healed over.

Above them, like a ceiling formed of raw magical power, was a pink shaded plane. The boulder suddenly cracked and half of it rolled a few dozen yards downhill.

Where the rock had just been, roots formed. Vanx had no idea what kind of tree it would be, but he knew a massive one was growing. This was the third of these gems he'd seen smashed. Before long, there would be a Heart Tree here, and its roots would work their way down into the earth and help bind the world, as the ancient towers the Paragon Dracus recently destroyed had once done.

It was odd that there were seven seeds, and only six towers, but who was Vanx to argue about what held the world together?

Where? came Poops's concerned question.

We are fine. Vanx responded. *Tell Gallarael we are going to slide downhill. Under the magic and start setting up a camp near the lake shore.*

Will, came the dog's response.

Vanx urged Chelda where he wanted her to go, and she complied. Before long, they were downslope enough that they could stand without crouching under the ever expanding plane of jewel dust.

"I told them we would start setting up a camp," he told Chelda.

"What do you think we will be looking for?" she asked, stooping to pick up a choice hunk of deadfall. "What did your Goddess say we were after?"

"She didn't," Vanx chuckled. "She said after we cracked that gem here, we would learn what we needed to know." He pointed to a semicircle formed of fir, or maybe pine trees. Their bark was always sticky with sap, but these were so close together that they formed a natural barrier, and the carpet of fallen needles beneath them would make for a fine bed. If they put themselves between those trunks, with a good sized fire, he was certain nothing would bother them in the night. Not while a massive magical tree formed just up the hill.

"The Goddess doesn't say much, does she?" Chelda jested and went about making a fire pit and collecting more wood.

A rustling in the thicket nearby caused them both to make ready. Gallarael, in her most human form, strolled out. Vanx thought she was beautiful, but still preferred her long natural blonde hair to the shoulder length black mop she'd been sporting since she'd gotten control of her shapeshifting. He wondered if she changed her hair, too? She must, because she hadn't cut it on the voyage and it was still as short as it was when they'd left.

She had explained to Vanx that, when she changed, her skin filmed over with a substance that she could either harden into a protective armor, or she could make the stuff become armoring spikes, or even strands of bristly fur. Vanx wasn't sure what happened to her clothes when she was changed, but Gallarael had taken to wearing loose fitting britches and a sleeveless blouse all of the time. When she was in human form, her apple sized breasts jiggled underneath the garment. It was distracting.

"I know I am attractive, my love," Gallarael jested, "but you don't have to stare."

"Sorry." Vanx shook his head and saw that the power of the ruby was dissipating. The plane of particles and magic slowly disappeared and, where the boulder had been, was the base of a growing tree. Vanx thought it might be a jacaranda tree, as it had the telltale purple bell shaped blooms sprouting in the higher reaches now. The branches were spreading out as much as they were growing upward.

One of the blooms fell and drifted slowly down. Vanx followed it with his eyes. He walked over to where it landed and was surprised to see that it was the size of a ship's bell. Similar blooms were coming down here and there, some three times the size of the one before him.

It was certainly a jacaranda tree, or a variation of one, Vanx decided. This tree's flowers were turning more red than blue, though.

He was distracted from his observations by the sound of Castovanti complaining.

"Last time we were here, this robe almost caused me to drown." He pointed to a cavern that opened on the water on the far side of the lake. "That hole is where Chelda and I killed those things." He stopped and looked at the gargan woman and Vanx in turn.

"Didn't we decide back then, that the shore of the lake was the worst place to set up a camp? I think Zeezle's exact words were, not there, sooner or later, every living thing on this island will come to get a drink."

"He did say something like that." Vanx gave a sarcastic snort. Castovanti had a knack for saying the wrong thing at the wrong time. "But that was before this just appeared." Vanx paused and pointed at the still growing, hundred foot tall tree. He nearly forgot he was telling the sea mage something when he saw just how red the tree's blooms were turning. They were getting yellowed tips too, like the Fiery Trees of lore. "What we just did scared the turds right out of anything living in this valley, man. But even still, we will only stay this one night."

"Tomorrow we go a questing," Gallarael sang one of the songs Vanx had often played when he was a simple preforming bard back in Cold Port. "A questing we will go. What we find and who survives, we won't know until we know."

"Leave the singing to the bard," Chelda said. "You're going to call in some wild beast looking to mate."

"Her voice is fine," Moonsy said as she and Poops came to stand near Vanx and take in the tree.

I know Poops, Vanx acknowledged the dog's two concerns. *We just have to suffer the smell of the flowers. There's naught to be done about it, and I am smart enough to keep my mouth shut about how bad she sings.*

"This kind of tree is supposed to have blue and purple flowers, not red and yellow," Moonsy said. "It will not grow any higher than the ridge either."

"Why not?" Castovanti asked, intentionally cutting off the verse Gallarael was about to go into.

"They do not like the salty air." The elven general sounded confident in her knowledge. "The fresh water, and the way it sits, rooted in the valley will help its lower reaches flourish though."

"Well that's good," Vanx sighed. "Not knowing what sort of tree each gem-seed contains makes it that much harder to pick a place to quicken them."

"The bluest flower petals, when added to a hot bath, are used to treat many things." Castovanti added as he gained Vanx's side. "I'm not sure what one colored as red as blood would do. Do you think I can take a sample to study?"

"Be careful," Vanx patted the timid man on the shoulder. "Goofing around with strange plants is how Gallarael became a changeling."

Chapter Three

> We're off to go a questing,
> a questing we will go.
> Who will live and who will die,
> only the Goddess knows.
> - A Tavern Song

Watches were set before they slept, but dawn came and went without a single one of the group stirring. Vanx woke, his skin wet with sweat. Poops woke too, immediately filling Vanx's mind and body with agitated worry.

Vanx had to fight his way out of the deep slumber, but when he did, he realized that the smell of the blooms was overpowering, and that it had to be what caused the drowsiness. It was so potent that Anitha and Castovanti, who had been the second watch, had fallen asleep by the fire pit.

Go drink and pee, Vanx let the dog tend his necessities. He didn't wake Gallarael when he got up and found a tree trunk to relieve himself on, but he started waking the rest of the group one by one when he was finished.

They were all groggy, and Anitha was so upset over falling asleep at her post that she started crying and begging her general to forgive her. Moonsy seemed annoyed by the elven spell caster's groveling but let her carry on. Castovanti wouldn't wake up so Vanx interrupted the apologetic elf.

"I think, because he is human, the pollen, or whatever it is, affected him worse." Vanx started to ask if Anitha had a spell, but he remembered that he still had the glaive clipped to his belt and stuck the man with it. A few minutes later, when Castovanti still hadn't stirred, he grew concerned.

"He isn't hurt, Vanx," Moonsy said, crawling from she and Chelda's bedroll. "The sword only heals. It doesn't wake people up."

"I was afraid he may be poisoned or something of that sort. He's just a human, after all."

"Just kick him," Chelda growled. She sat up, stretched her arms out and yawned. Her huge breasts, pressed against her normally loose fitting, tattered blouse for a moment, causing her nipples to be pronounced against it. It might have stirred something in Vanx had he not looked upon her as he would a sister.

"Where in all the hells, is Papri?" Vanx asked, looking at Moonsy and Anitha in turn. Anitha was still upset so he tried to console her. "It wasn't your fault the blooms affected us in such a way," Vanx said. "Don't beat yourself up over it."

"I have wards to protect me...us against such things, sir." She bowed her head in his direction. "I will be more vigilant next time. The Troika Sven allowed Papri and I to come, to protect the—" she paused to stifle a yawn, "glaive. Someone could have strolled right into our camp and taken it."

"There is no one here to steal it." Vanx rubbed her hair like he might a youngster. "See if you can reach out to Papri or the hawks."

"Yes." She nodded and stepped away to find a place to go about her business.

"I will see if I can wake Castovanti," Moonsy said. Her golden yellow hair looked like a bird nest that had slid halfway off a branch. He was certain his brown mop wasn't much better.

Vanx looked where Gallarael had just been, but she was gone. Panic threatened to overtake his tired mind. Then, through his familiar link with Poops, he felt her approaching. A calming wave washed over him. A glance in their direction told him she was going to the water to fill some canteens and probably give the pup his usual morning belly rub. He was just glad she looked human. She had achieved so much control over her shapeshifting that she could transform, in progressions, all the way into the strange feline thing she sometimes was. But she could stay half formed, or quarter formed, too, and climb, leap, and fight like a pack of acrobatic badgers.

It only took a few moments for Moonsy to get Castovanti to open his eyes, but what Anitha said sucked away all the relief Vanx felt.

"Papri isn't responding." The elf's voice was full of concern. "The great hawks aren't either. I did sense one of them, but what it was emoting was so sorrowful that I couldn't bear it." She looked at Moonsy and then Vanx, fighting back more tears. The concern in her expression was bordering on dire.

Vanx started to suggest something, but hope wiped away Anitha's look. "Wait." she held up a hand to belay Vanx's comment. "One of them is coming now. They are birds and not as sentient as other creatures, but I think it knows where the others are. It isn't the sad one."

"I'd bet the pollen got them, too," Moonsy said, helping Castovanti sit up and sip from her water skin.

"I hope—" Castovanti started, and Vanx wondered what sort of untimely comment the man was about to make. Castovanti didn't disappoint, either. After he took another sip, he finished. "I hope Papri and his—his bird weren't too high in the air when they lost their senses."

"By the Lanch and Lecher themselves." Chelda jumped to her feet. "I'll slap your farkin' jaw off if you don't stop doing that." The nature of her swearing was lost to all but Vanx, and maybe Moonsy. Avia Lanch was the witch that caused snow banks to tumble down from the mountains, and the Lecher was the deviant mythical creature who snatched little girls that strayed too far from the gargan village Chelda grew up in.

Vanx did know that, when she invoked both evils in one curse, she was about to get violent.

"Enough!" Vanx barked, hoping to quell her anger.

Poops sensed the approaching great hawk as a rabbit might sense an owl about to grasp it from the ground. Vanx sensed the same thing, through the pup, and turned just in time to get a face full of dust and pine needles. The big bird had dropped right down among them. The back-flapping of its wings stirred leaves and debris as it slowed its descent and landed.

Before Vanx could tell Anitha to mount the creature, Moonsy leapt to its shoulders and placed her forehead against its feathery neck. Vanx had come to understand this was a way of pairing their minds so that they could fly and fight in concert. A moment later, they lifted into the sky.

Vanx, now concerned that they'd already lost someone, made his way over to the lake to rinse away the crud stuck to his damp skin. He didn't go where Gallarael and Poops were, because he wanted to take a peek at the piece of the Mirror of Portent. It wasn't until he reached for it that he remembered that he'd given it to Zeezle.

Cursing himself for not bringing it along, he pulled off the sark he was wearing, and went about cleansing his upper body.

Before he could finish, Anitha was calling them, her voice as full of anguish as it was excitement.

"Moonsy found them," Anitha yelled. "She found Papri and his hawk. They are tangled in the trees, in a bad way. The other hawk was there, but it fled when it saw her." She took a breath and wiped at her eyes. "Moonsy is returning for the glaive." The emotional elf then fell to her knees, put her head in her hands, and started crying in earnest.

Chapter Four

*The half-demon wizard, Pael,
he tried to kill them all.
Only a handful got away,
and Wildermont did fall.*
-The Ballad of Ornspike

"What about the other hawk? Why did it flee?" Castovanti asked.

"Stow it," Vanx commanded sharply from across the distance between he and the camp. He closed his eyes a moment and used Poops's senses to locate the approaching bird again. Grabbing the Hoar Witch's crystal hanging at his neck, he called out to Moonsy, and then hurled the glaive high into the air.

The great hawk's shadow slid over them an instant before Moonsy and the hawk did. To Vanx's grim satisfaction, the bird canted to the side, and the elven general grabbed the hilt of the slowly arcing blade as they passed.

"Yah," he heard Chelda say, but Vanx knew she was admiring the throw and catch, not seconding Vanx telling the sea mage to hold his tongue.

Vanx started to say something to Gallarael, but she was gone. Poops came loping back to the camp, one of the canteens clutched awkwardly in his jaws. He dropped it at Vanx's feet and sat. Vanx took the moment, dropped to his knees, and tried to clear the haze from his mind while petting the dog. He wished he had a way to contact Ronzon on the *Adventurer*. Maybe the other hawk would return there and light on the mast or the figurehead Chelda had carved, as they often had when they were crossing the sea.

"Oh no." Anitha's visible sadness was suddenly gone. "General Moonseed was too late."

Vanx was hardened to death. It was part of adventuring, but Papri hadn't really chosen this adventure. The seven ancient elves that made up the Troika Sven had chosen his fate for him. And the hawks, well, Vanx wasn't sure he liked the way the elves manipulated the otherwise mostly wild creatures, but it had to do with elven magic and the Heart Tree so he had no choice but to accept it.

"Papri, or the hawk, or both?" Castovanti asked. He'd moved a good distance away from Chelda, Vanx noticed. The man glared at her and looked as if he had a spell on the tip of his tongue, just in case she tried to smack him. "It is a valid question." He looked at Vanx for support.

It was a valid question.

"Tell us, Anitha," Vanx said, giving Chelda a look. Chelda actually liked the fact that Castovanti wasn't letting her bully him. Vanx understood her all too well. Neither of them felt sadness over this sort of loss, just the regret that a companion was no longer with them.

"Both," Anitha dropped her head again, but after a second she heaved in a breath and let it out slowly. "They are not that far away. We should go help her get them down."

Castovanti started to speak, but held his tongue. Instead, he, too, started grabbing up his overnight gear. He didn't have much to gather because he never got in his bedroll. After a moment, he stopped and did ask something. "Do we have time for me to get out of this robe? It just isn't practical to wear a robe in the woods."

"He's learning, Vanxy," Chelda said. "It ain't practical to wear a robe on a ship either, but all you creepy wizards seem to think it is."

"Don't dally, man." Vanx nodded, noticing that Chelda and Moonsy's gear was already bundled and stowed in Chelda's big backpack.

"Vanx," Gallarael's voice called from the forest around the lakeshore a bit. "You have to see this!"

Poops tore off in that direction, his tongue lolling out of his mouth, and his nubbed tail wiggling back and forth as if all of life was just a game. Chelda followed the dog.

"After you've changed, come after us," Vanx said. "You can come or wait on him," he told Anitha, who nodded.

"I'm going Castov," Anitha said when Vanx jogged away. "I'll walk slow so you can still see me when you are done."

*

Vanx saw Gallarael, and was again glad she was in human form. Once when they were deep into a night of carnal pleasure, she'd shifted just a bit. Not so much her body, but her rhythm, and her eyes had gone wild, and Vanx was torn out of the moment by the happening. Still, he loved her, or thought he did.

"What is it?" he called out as he gained Chelda's side.

"Just come look." Gallarael smiled as he and Chelda drew near. Poops was already there, sniffing at something rather large, which was fast asleep, and covered in gray-green skin. "Is this what was making those prints you told me about?"

"No, Poops," Vanx said sharply when he saw what it was. "Never lick a toad, pup. Some of them have oil on their skin that will make you see your maker and melt like a candle."

"Do you think he understands all of that?" Gallarael asked. "He's just curious."

"Papri and his bird are dead," Chelda said. "If you didn't hear."

"I gathered as much," Gallarael nodded. "He— They will be missed."

Vanx listened absently as he took in what he first thought was a frog of sorts. It was no frog though, or maybe it was part frog. It was half the size of his ship, and it had frog-like skin and a toadish head. It was a four-legged creature though, with what looked like webbed paws. It didn't seem natural, yet here it was, hanging around the freshwater shore just like a frog would.

"Well, that is one less thing to keep me awake at night," Castovanti said as he and Anitha joined them.

"He said something that wasn't stupid." Chelda looked perplexed.

"Anitha, can you try and summon the hawk that fled, again?" Vanx asked. "I'd like for someone to get a bird's eye view of the island and see what else the new Heart Tree has put to sleep."

This caused them all to look back at the now massive jacaranda Heart Tree they'd quickened. The bell shaped flowers were scattered in clusters that seemed like impossible clouds, formed in hues of purple, red, and yellow.

Not even Castovanti could find words.

Anitha found some, though. "My dear friend has just died." Her tone was severe. "With all due respect, Vanx of Malic, can we please go help the general."

"Yah." Chelda slapped Vanx on the shoulder and indicated that Anitha could lead the way.

Chapter Five

> Good old Master Wiggins,
> grew too old to dance.
> He still came to festival,
> but he forgot to wear his pants.
> - A Parydonian Street Ditty

The sun had passed overhead. Now, it wasn't far from setting behind the ridge of the bowl-shaped valley cradling the lake. When Vanx finally saw the scattered feathers, and then the twisted wings, he felt guilty for not feeling anything more than he did. He hoped Papri and the bird died from the impact, instead of suffering, but if they'd been unconscious from the tree's pollen, maybe they hadn't felt the pain the sight of their end portrayed.

Moonsy was on the ground, a streak of crackling yellow energy that made the hair on Vanx's neck stand up, was lifting Papri's broken form away from where it was wedged in a fork of limbs. The tree was an older strain of oak that had risen high above the forest. By the look of the ground around the determined elven general, her magic had cut an unforgiving path to get to him. Broken limbs of all sizes, some smoldering from her arcanery, some still full of bright green leaves, were scattered all around her.

Anitha and Castovanti ran past Vanx and Chelda. Vanx had hoped to see Gallarael, but she was nowhere in sight.

"Look." Chelda pointed.

Moonsy was lowering Papri's body slowly to the ground. Below the corpse, Anitha and Castovanti had joined their power to Moonsy's. Vanx didn't think

Moonsy needed assistance but the gesture was what it was.

When the dead elf was settled on the turf, Castovanti started doing the same sort of thing to the great hawk. Anitha joined him, but Moonsy was mothering over Papri's form. Vanx knew she was hardened, too, but maybe not so much as he and Chelda. The great wars against the Hoar Witch, and then the Trigon, had taken their toll on all the peoples of their side of the world, especially the fae.

"Set up camp?" Chelda asked.

"Yup." Vanx pointed to the trunk of the grand oak their companions had crashed into. There was a place at the base of the massive tree that looked like perfect shelter.

"Yah." Chelda nodded her agreement and went about collecting deadfall.

Vanx stood there a moment. He started to help Chelda, but a thought occurred to him. Back on Three Tower Island, Anitha had cast a spell to determine where the ruby gem-seed was hidden. He decided to see what Moonsy thought before he interrupted the untangling of the hawk. She needed the distraction anyway.

Vanx grabbed the crystal hanging at his neck and directed his thought voice to Moonsy alone. *Can Anitha cast a detection spell and help us get on with this before anyone else gets hurt?*

On Papri's map there is a structure. We might not be the only two-legged folk out here, came her response.

Vanx looked over at her more closely. She wasn't mothering. She'd unrolled a map on Papri's chest and was studying it from her knees.

Vanx went over to see it for himself, but she continued as he came.

It is probably long deserted, but since the island somehow maintains its invisibility, maybe whoever made this place so hard to find is still here. She looked up and forced a smile when Vanx came around and squatted beside her. Poops put his head between them and sniffed at Papri. He let out a little whine, before easing back and turning a circle. Only then did he lay down and put his chin on his forepaws.

"Or maybe whatever else is here was hidden from the world for good reasons." Vanx looked at the map. "I only found this island because a crazy old wizard sent me. His map is down in that hole where Zeezle almost bought the farmhouse. The hole was here." Vanx pulled a lead marker from the dead elf's pocket and made an "X" where he wanted it. Papri had done excellent work but something struck him immediately.

"Why would he buy a farm hou—" Moonsy started, but Vanx cut her off.

"Look." He pointed at the map. "What are these? They look like stream beds, or the like. See, no trees," Vanx pointed at three areas leading away from the rectangle marked *unknown structure*. "But the building's elevation suggests it is higher and close to the sea. So why are there no trees in these, these—?"

"Lanes?" Moonsy suggested so softly Vanx wasn't sure she intended to think out loud. A heartbeat later, she looked up at Vanx as if she'd had some revelation, then she stood, bringing herself eye to eye with him.

"Anitha, let Castovanti finish that." Moonsy called the order, like the general she was. "We need you here."

Anitha came quickly, her elven stride, and the way she kept wiping at her nose, made her seem like a child. When she got there and saw that they were using Papri's body as a map table, she nearly lost her composure. Moonsy's commanding tone brought her out of it.

"Cast your most variant detection." Moonsy pointed at the structure, and the treeless lanes Papri had sketched. "Concentrate on these areas here. If you have to go to the ridge, take Chelda and Castovanti both, and be back before darkfall."

"I'll try from here first. It doesn't look to be that far." Anitha seemed confident in her ability. "If there isn't too much ore in these ridges, it will be easy."

27

Anitha took the map and gave Moonsy a side look as she moved to another place and sat down cross legged with the map in front of her.

Vanx watched as she made a few gestures, and then spoke a word. The map glowed and Anitha's eyes closed for a moment, then the spell was done.

Vanx stood as the spell caster fluttered her eyelids and shook her head. "There is magic in the structure, deep below it anyway. But those paths are of concern."

Anitha got to her feet and brought Papri's map back to her commander. "As you said, General, I'll need to go to the ridge to get a better feel for what that is all about, but I'm sure they are significant, for they each extend all the way to the sea."

Vanx dropped to his knees and looked at the map again. He looked for the hole he and Zeezle had went down and found the "X" he'd just made. "They divide the island into three parts, and we've only ever been in this section, he showed them. Find out what they are, Anitha, but be careful. Let Chelda lead you to the ridge, and do what she says." Vanx was stern. "She is good at this." He gestured at the wilderness around them.

"I appreciate your concern Master Vanx," Anitha gave Moonsy a look. "But I've been alive for almost two hundred years. I'm pretty good at this, too."

Vanx stretched his mouth wide and nodded. "She's still going with you, but not Castovanti. Chelda might smash his head flat if he says the wrong thing."

No one could argue that.

Chapter Six

> The king saw the wizard,
> and the wizard had a grin.
> Your kingdom is collapsing, said the mage.
> Your reign has found its end.
> -The Weary Wizard

Anitha followed Chelda up the grade, but it was Sir Poopsalot who was really in the lead. Chelda had to restrain her gait so Anitha could keep up. She was used to it, for she and Moosy took walks in the forest when they could. Chelda looked back at the elf and decided that, though Anitha was dark haired, dark complected, and beautiful, she felt no attraction, or maybe she did, only her attraction to Moonsy was so powerful it smothered anything else. That was it, Chelda decided. That had to be it.

Another thing that lingered in her mind was the way Vanx had glanced at her breasts the previous morning. It didn't bother her that he'd looked. In fact, she'd felt flattered for his bright green eyes and bardish roguery drew all sorts of beautiful women to him. The fact he'd bothered to pause, and stare, for even a slight a moment, made her feel attractive. The problem was, him looking had made something new tingle deep inside her. There was no doubt she loved Moonsy and hated most men, but Vanx was anything but most men.

Soon, they topped the rise, and Chelda relished the feel of the fresh wind they found. The cool air made its way to her sweaty body through her torn up blouse and dried her skin quickly. It also blew her ponderings away and seemed to clear some of the sleepiness from her mind. It wasn't the breeze that struck her most, though. She'd half-expected to see more ocean before them, but they were on nearly the opposite side of the lake from where they'd arrived, and another valley spread out below. This one still had the sun almost fully upon it, but the far ridge of this depression was in shadow, and who knew what lay beyond.

The treetops were a lush carpet of every shade of green imaginable, and the forest was littered with bright, red-leaved trees, that seemed to command some space between themselves and the rest of the jungly vegetation. There was what looked like a road hewn through the dense growth, though, and Chelda saw that, in the farthest reaches of her vision, the road led to what might have been a large, low built castle.

"I hope we aren't going there," she said out loud. *It would be a hell of a trek to get this group through all of that green shit,* she thought. When she heard no response, she turned to see that Anitha was deep in her spell casting.

The elf was focused in concentration and moving her hands around crazily, as spell casters sometimes do. Chelda didn't like magic, but she wasn't afraid of it. She just didn't understand it.

"Poops," Chelda called to keep the dog from roaming too far down into the thicket. "Come on, Poops. Come see your Chelly Chel."

Poops returned and Chelda squatted down to give him some attention while she waited. It wasn't until Poops stiffened and started growling that she saw what had him agitated.

There was a bird, one of the great hawks, winging its way over from the opposite ridge. It was hard to see against the shadow thrown from the setting sun, but she followed it as it grew nearer. She assumed it was the great hawk that fled. Poops clearly didn't think so, and Chelda suddenly remembered the winged creature that snatched that big coonish thing from a tree when they were here the first time.

"Anitha," Chelda said, seeing now that it wasn't their friendly hawk, but a larger predator, maybe a roc. "Anitha, enough!" Chelda spoke sharply. Poops

The Legend of Vanx Malic

added a warning bark of his own, and when Anitha still didn't pull herself out of her spell, the dog left Chelda, went over and nudged her with his head.

"What?" she grumbled. "I'm sensing something."

Chelda looked back and was suddenly nervous. The creature was gone.

"There is something out there flying around." Chelda made sure her voice conveyed her concern. "It ain't one of the hawks either."

"I believe you." Anitha sucked in an audible breath of air and faced Chelda as she let it out slowly. "I have to tell Vanx. That is no river bed, or road over there. It is an area scorched of life by magic. That structure is—"

Poops exploded into a fit of barking, and an ear-piercing screech cut through the evening. A winged creature covered in purple-black feathers dropped out of nowhere. Anitha's whole head fit into one of its claws, and Chelda imagined the poor elf's neck snapping when the child sized elf was yanked violently from the ridge. The giant roc, or raven, or whatever it was, was leaving with Anitha dangling helplessly from its claw.

Chelda grabbed her war hammer by the handle, took a long stride to add momentum to her throw, and hurled it as hard as she could.

Poops made all sorts of noise. Chelda felt just like the dog sounded, and when her hammer impacted the bird, the creature faltered, but not enough to bring it down.

Chelda's heart sank. Not only did they lose another member of their group, Anitha had just discovered something…something she'd needed to tell Vanx.

Chelda watched where her hammer landed, but before she could start after it, another shriek filled her ears, this one was from one of the great hawks, for she recognized the sound immediately.

Instinctively, she dropped to her knees. She watched raptly as the great hawk shot across the treetops and got a hold of the black bird's head and neck. The raven was half again bigger than the hawk was, and it didn't look like this was going to help Anitha, no matter what the birds did.

Size didn't seem to matter, for the hawk was fierce. It used its claws to twist the other's neck until it snapped. The big black raven dropped the elf and fell right out of the sky. Chelda stood and visored her eyes so she could see where Anitha landed. Once she marked where the elf should have ended up, she went after the war hammer while Poops went after the elf.

Chapter Seven

> A battle they did fight,
> across the land and in the sky.
> Against dragons and dark demon,
> by the thousands they did die.
> -The Ballad of Ornspike

By the time Chelda reached Anitha, she could hear some of the others trudging toward them. No doubt Poops had conveyed what was happening to Vanx, or maybe Vanx had been watching the whole thing through the dog's eyes? Either Vanx or Moonsy had the Glaive of Gladiolus, though, and Anitha desperately needed its healing power for she had a puncture wound in her neck that was spurting indigo colored blood in thick pulses.

"Draw the glaive," Chelda yelled as loud as she could. "And hurry."

Vanx arrived a second before Moonsy did. He fell beside Anitha and ran the edge of the ancient healing sword across her forearm. Moonsy fell beside her fellow elf and sobbed.

"She has lost too much," Moonsy sobbed. "Look at all the blood."

There was a puddle of liquid life, its hue more purple than red, and darkening the longer it sat. Chelda watched, trying to detach herself from what was happening. It didn't look good, for even though Anitha had been affected by the glaive, she still looked gray and as limp as a fresh corpse.

"No." Vanx's tone was soothing. "She will survive."

Anitha moaned then. "Vanx, there is—"

"No don't try to talk just yet," Moonsy poured water from a canteen on Anitha and cleansed some of the blood from her neck. The critical wound was already scabbing over and on its way to forming into scar tissue.

When Gallarael stepped out of the forest, still in the process of changing from thing to person, Chelda almost smashed her with the war hammer. Her people hated changelings. If she hadn't grown so close to Gallarael as a person, she wouldn't keep company with her, but they shared a love of Poops and Vanx and had gone through too much for Chelda to allow her childhood fears to control their friendship. Even still, Gallarael had almost gotten her pretty gourd flattened, for surprising them like that.

Chelda didn't miss the look of disgust when it flashed across Vanx's face as he saw her, and she suddenly understood something about their relationship.

"There is something inside that structure," Anitha said after taking a sip of water. "There are things that might be gah-guah-guarding it, too."

"And those roads are where magic shunned the forest back," Chelda added, happy that Anitha was coming around.

Vanx looked at Chelda, and then back at Anitha.

Chelda followed his eyes, and saw that their friend was getting some color back in her flesh.

"She's correct." Anitha took the canteen from Moonsy and drank deeply twice, before elaborating. "The island seems to be divided into three areas by a magical field that is still active."

"What sort of magic?" Moonsy asked.

"Ancient human magic, or the like," Anitha said, as if this was the worst sort of magic there was. "But I couldn't say for certain. I only know it isn't elven magic."

"Anything else?" Moonsy asked. This time the concern in her voice had dissipated. She sounded like a general again. A general asking for a report from a subordinate.

"At least two creatures emitting a detectable signature were near the structure. One in each section, only the area we are in now seems void of such a thing.

"Well that's good," Gallarael said, easing down beside the fallen elf to help Moonsy clean her up.

"I wonder why there is no creature in this section?" Vanx said. "I mean, there were those crabs, the spiders, and that thing that almost snatched Zeezle away in the boreholes. What could there be in those other areas that is worse?"

"Don't forget that four-legged frog-skinned thing down by the lake." Gallarael said. "It might not have been so pleased about us being here had the Heart Tree not put it to sleep."

"Believe me, Vanx," Anitha said. "Take it from someone who was almost killed by a hungry bird."

Don't fuck with the birds, Poops voiced to Vanx. It was something they'd decided when they were stranded in Harthgar, and Vanx had to fight back a laugh. Anitha was still talking, though, so he contained himself.

"—are things on this island we do not want to come across." She looked to be almost back to herself, now. "After a night's rest, I can teleport us from the ridge to very near the structure, but I won't try to teleport through one of those barriers."

"The birds have flown over them," Vanx said. "Remember, brave Papri mapped details from the other sides of the magical fields. They are passable, in the air, at least."

"Maybe so." Moonsy looked at Vanx. "Whoever created them could have allowed for nature though. Until we get a closer look, we won't be going through them."

"No, I agree." He took Anitha's hand and helped her to her feet. "But on the morrow, I want us to do as you suggested and teleport there."

"Yah." Chelda nodded. She hadn't wanted to go to the building because she'd thought they'd have to trudge through all that jungle to get there. Teleporting was creepy, and caused a feeling like thousands of ants crawling on her skin but, even so, to get there in an instant was another thing altogether. Now she was eager.

Chelda was relieved that Anitha was on her feet, but the whole way back down to their camp she had the feeling of something about to grab her from above. Even the thick canopy of trees between her and the open sky didn't alleviate the concern.

Only when Moonsy eased to her side, and hugged her thigh, did she stop feeling like prey.

When they came near the laid out bodies of Papri and his great hawk, sadness started to get a hold of Chelda, but then she noticed that the mouthy sea mage was nowhere to be seen. Since she knew he wasn't capable of surviving long on his own, she grew concerned.

"Where is Castovanti." Anitha stole the question from her tongue. "I don't see him anywhere."

Sorrow over Papri's loss evaporated in an instant, as all of them started calling his name. Right before their eyes, Gallarael shifted into her feline form and darted away.

Vanx made a sour face but said something to Poops, who ran off the other direction.

It was Chelda who spotted the fresh blood trail. It led about twenty paces out of the camp and was bright and frothy, as if the sea mage had been running. The splashes of scarlet, and his bootprints, ended abruptly. A look up told Chelda that no bird could have gotten him, but the sight of a score or more man-sized, coon-tailed creatures up in the trees, and the tattered bloody clothes dangling from a few different limbs told Chelda all she needed to know.

They'd eaten him, Chelda understood. They probably tore him apart while he was alive, to do so.

Anitha, having looked up and seen the gore that remained, dangling like pieces of crimson stained rope, fell to her knees sobbing.

"He is here," Chelda told the others. "Was here, I mean."

"Why didn't they go after Papri or the great hawk?" Anitha asked Vanx and Moonsy when they came jogging up.

"Probably because they like fresh meat," Chelda answered for them.

Chapter Eight

> All ends will have beginnings,
> and each one will be new.
> Where you go, when you reach the end,
> is only up to you.
> - A tavern song

Vanx was angry at himself for leaving the unseasoned sea mage alone with two carcasses that had surely been drawing in carrion. Moonsy blasted up at the tree-coons with powerful spells. It was overkill, for the little elven general set the whole tree top off with sticky elven wizard fire. Anitha gathered herself and picked off the ring-tailed creatures that were fleeing as best as she could.

"Well, everything on the island knows where we are now," Vanx sighed.

"If there is anyone paying attention," Gallarael would have startled him, but Poops's keen sense of smell warned him of her approach before her voice was in his ear, "they'd have to know we were here since we unleashed the Heart Tree."

"True." Vanx turned and saw that she looked like her beautiful self, minus the long golden hair he'd liked so much. The depth of her eyes made him forget how unsettling it was to see her shifting, or shifted. The only two forms of her he felt comfortable with were her natural appearance, and her fully formed panther-like form. The in between was instinctively repulsive.

"We have a pillar of smoke rising out of our camp though." He pointed to where Moonsy had opened the canopy up. It wasn't full dark yet, but almost. Around all the smoldering greenery, he could see bright stars.

Oddly, he found himself wondering if Ronzon had caught any fish. Then he wondered if there were any fish in the lake they'd rooted the Heart Tree near. When they were finished with their business here, maybe he would wet his line.

He helped Chelda rig some intrusion bells and argued with Anitha about her setting up protective wards. She needed rest. She'd nearly died, and Vanx had no desire to be teleported into a tree trunk, on the morrow, by a spell weary caster.

The four remaining members of their party set up watches. Vanx had the last, which was fine with him, for he rose early most days anyway. He didn't get to sleep through until his turn though, for Moonsy and Poops both went off in the middle of the night.

Everyone exploded into readiness, and only after the returned great hawk let out a screech of protest, did they belay their weapons and spells.

Vanx tried, but couldn't fall back into slumber. He relieved Moonsy, when the time came, and spent most of the pre-dawn scratching Sir Poopsalot behind the ears while contemplating why the old wizard who had helped him in Harthgar hadn't explained more about this place. He wished he still had the wizard's map, but he'd dropped it when he was defending Zeezle in the bore-worm hole. At least that is where he thought he'd dropped it.

Vanx, sighed. They could have explored all of this when they were here the first time.

Vanx decided that Anitha and Moonsy were better equipped for this kind of task. Where he and Zeezle used their physical agility and natural Zythian instinct to achieve their end, the elves used powerful magic. On an island like this, one was definitely safer than the other. They'd already lost two of their small group, and the rest had barely arrived. Zeezle had almost died when they were here last time, and if it weren't for the Glaive of Gladiolus, Zeezle, nor Anitha would have made it.

Better with them, Poops conveyed.

"I have to agree," Vanx answered in a whisper.

"Agree with what?" Gallarael asked as she sat beside him. "Are you talking to that pooch again?"

"Yup." Vanx smiled at her. He wondered where the night had gone, for the sky was already starting to pink with the hope of dawn.

"I wonder why those things didn't try to eat Papri?" Gallarael's question was serious.

"I think either they don't like the taste of elves or they only like a fresh kill."

"The latter most like." She slid closer, put her arm around him, and leaned her head against his shoulder.

"I can sense it, when my changing repulses you, love." Gallarael's voice was soft and understanding. "It is a natural thing to be put off. It is like the dragon fear, or the sleepiness caused by that Heart Tree we just rooted. But it hurts me to know that part of my being makes you feel so."

"I can't control it, Gal." Vanx shrugged. "I don't want to feel ill when I see you that way. It just happens."

"That's what I'm saying." She turned him to face her. "You didn't want to feel fear when you came near Pyra, but you did, even though you knew she loved you."

"I wasn't afra—"

"Yes," Gallarael kissed him quickly. "You were afraid every instant you were near that dragon."

Vanx had to admit she was right. Even after long conversations with the wyrm, and after the great red fire queen trusted him enough to allow him into her lair, he'd been scared of her. How could you not be afraid of something that had teeth as big as you were.

Then Vanx understood.

He never was really afraid of the dragon, save for their first meeting, but Pyra radiated fear all the time. Just like he wasn't repulsed by Gallarael at the moment. At the moment, the taste of her kiss was sweet and still on his lips. But if she were to change, his attraction would be replaced by disgust.

Maybe he didn't understand, but he knew he loved her when she was in human form. He didn't even mind that she was a changeling, as long as he didn't have to see her shifting shapes. It was the changing, or maybe something her body emitted while she was changing, that made him feel the way he did.

He gave her a hug and indicated that he needed to visit the trees. To his surprise, she went with him and, after kissing him ardently, half hidden in the shadows, she dropped to her knees, took him in her mouth, and satisfied him.

Nothing about that made him feel repulsed, he decided while hugging a trunk to keep himself standing. Nothing at all.

Chapter Nine

> I picked a special flower,
> to make my Molly purr,
> but right after she kissed me,
> she said two coppers sir.
> – Parydon Cobbles

The sun was above the ridge when they were finally situated and ready for Anitha to cast her teleport spell. The elf had ridden the great hawk just after dawn and gotten a closer look at the terrain and the structure they would be appearing near.

It was only when they were all huddled together that Vanx realized he was the only male left on the island. Papri, and Castovanti were dead, leaving three women with him. Ronzon was still guarding the ship, he remembered. To manage the ship, he would need a man's strength— No, he changed his mind. Chelda was stronger than Ronzon was, but Ronzon knew the rigging and, without him Vanx would have to rely on his strange connection with the ship.

Me, Poops conveyed, reminding Vanx that he was a male, too.

Vanx started to respond with his mind, but Anitha's spell suddenly wrapped itself around them and they were standing in a much drier climate. The stickiness of the jungle terrain was gone, and though the forest here was as lush and full of life, the undergrowth hadn't taken over.

The air was cooler and dry, but still strongly tinged with brine. Vanx had to bite back a chuckle when he saw the way Chelda was batting and swatting at her skin. When he oriented himself to the cardinal directions, he saw one of the building's outer walls and followed it to where it made a corner.

For the briefest of moments, he thought he saw a head pull back around the edge, as if someone was watching them, but the salty wind caused a tree limb to waver and the shadow appeared, then disappeared on the edge of the wall again. It was what he'd seen, for the limb's silhouette looked just like a sneak trying to get out of sight.

The wall itself was fairly plain. Constructed of gray stone blocks, it was two stories tall at best, and might have been only one. The roof only had the slightest pitch to it, just enough to let the rain wash away. Vanx saw where one of the long empty clearings ran off to the right in a straight line. The area they were in, and immediately around the building seemed devoid of life, too.

Looking around, he saw that behind them, another lane of grassless dirt led away until it topped a ridge and disappeared from view.

"What can you tell me about it?" Vanx asked. "The building itself seems to be holding the forest, even the grass back, just like the lanes are, and we're right in it."

"There is strong power flowing from inside, and the lanes are boun—"

Just then Poops chased a darting rabbit across the empty stretch Vanx looked at. The dog ran, and when he came to the center of the lane, his snout, followed by the rest of his body, were stopped flat. A ripple of wavering sparkles made clear there was a barrier there. The way Poops yelped, and sent pain burning through Vanx's body, Vanx knew they couldn't just walk through.

Vanx jogged over to the startled dog, who was now ignoring his pain and growling at the rabbit, that had passed right through. The fat hopper sat there munching the petals of a bright yellow flower, as if it knew the dog could no longer get at it. It had to have eluded predators this way before. Vanx eased down near his familiar and began soothing his four-legged friend. He guessed the varmints that were of the island weren't stopped by the barrier, thus the rabbits and birds were able to pass freely.

"You'll get him next time." Vanx told the dog. "It's all right, pup. If I had a bow, I'd shaft the little bastard just for teasing you."

A roar, as loud and primal as that made by a full grown dragon, resounded from what Poops sensed was just on the other side of the building. It was so loud and savage that Poops forgot the rabbit and darted behind Vanx.

"Scaredy Pooch," Chelda teased, but her eyes were open so wide Vanx thought she might strain a brow. She had the war hammer out, too, but Vanx knew that it would take more than Chelda and her hammer to stop whatever made that sound.

"Let me see Papri's map," Vanx asked while trying to gather himself.

"Was it a dragon?" Anitha asked.

"Use your spells," Moonsy ordered. "I need you to cast every detection you know. Magic, evil, creatures, witchborn; all of them."

"Are we sure that, that—" Vanx indicated the thing that had made the noise, "can't get at us here?"

"I'm pretty sure," Anitha gave Vanx, and then Moonsy, a look. "I'm about to know all I can know about this area and what is in it."

"Look." Gallarael pointed down the lane, to a point farther than the best archer Vanx knew might be able to put an arrow. There, a sizable herd of antelope, tentatively crossed the open stretch, strolling right through the barrier that had stopped his dog.

Vanx watched raptly as none of them were affected by the field. To the animals, it wasn't even there. Then the giant shadow of an avian predator slid across the antelope still in the open, and they bolted after their fellows.

Vanx saw it was one of the two great hawks and an idea struck him.

"Moonsy," he asked, taking her concentration off of Anitha. "Can you see through the eyes of the hawks? Or better yet can you mount one and see what made that sound? It had to be, probably still is, not far beyond." He indicated the building.

"She can, but she will need rest first," Moonsy seemed miffed by something. "My duty is to protect the glaive, not any of this other stuff. Though I don't like it, I must not stray too far from your side, Vanx." She forced a smile. "This place isn't right." She shrugged. "I have a bad feeling."

"Yah," Chelda agreed. "Where is Gal?"

Vanx looked around and didn't see her. He let out a sigh and tried to ignore everything just for a moment. He was sure he was missing something.

How could the rabbit and the deer pass, but not a dog?

Maybe it was because Poops was his familiar and they shared a magical bond?

While they waited for Anitha to finish, and Gallarael to return from wherever she'd gone, Vanx pondered the issue, but nothing came to him.

He was brought out of his deep thoughts when Poops nudged him. Anitha was about to explain what she'd sensed to Moonsy and Chelda, and Vanx wanted to hear exactly what she had to say.

Chapter Ten

> From the open sea the spire it grew,
> and pointed toward the midnight sky.
> But nothing else did that old spike do,
> as a million years passed by.
> – a sailors song

Anitha said something to her general and then Moonsy asked Vanx for the glaive. After poking the exhausted elven spell caster, she returned it to Vanx. They gave her a moment to gather herself, then listened as she told them what she'd perceived from her detection spells.

"There is something inanimate inside those walls. It is so powerful I can feel it through the ground itself." Anitha paused seemingly contemplating her thoughts. "Why the island is divided, I cannot say, but I have no doubt that there are creatures outside this place, here to guard whatever is inside, for they are magicked, too. They are actually bound to the prize, so to speak, so I imagine whatever it is in there will be a help to our cause. I sensed something else on the southernmost end of the island, too, but we are too far away for me to detect anything specific about it."

Anitha scratched her head. Vanx thought she looked like a girl caught in indecision, as if she were trying to decide between the apple or the cherry pie.

"No doubt the answers you seek will be in this place."

"What makes you so sure of that, Anni," Moonsy asked. "How do you know?"

"I can't be fully certain, but there is nothing else radiating this powerful kind of magic on the island that I can tell." She took a deep sip from her canteen and continued.

"Is it another Heart Tree jewel you are sensing inside there?" Vanx asked.

"The object isn't a gem-seed, and it isn't just behind those walls, either." She pointed at the building, then her index finger started lowering. "What you are after Vanx, is below it. I can tell there are rooms and halls, below where we are now standing, even. Whatever is in there is far more powerful than one of the gems. There are probably wards and all sorts of peril inside as well as outside."

"So there isn't a gem-seed in each section?" Vanx was a little let down. He was hoping to find the last three gem-seeds, with instructions. He was also hoping it would be as easy as getting the other two had been. If there was one in each section, and something inside the structure, with an indication of where they should be cracked, he might not have felt so discouraged.

"It's time to go a questing. A questing we will go," Gallarael sang badly as she eased out of the forest on the side of the barrier Poops's rabbit had run to. "What we find, and who'll survive, soon enough we'll know."

"How did you get—" Anitha's question was drowned out by Vanx asking the exact same thing.

"How did you get over there?" Vanx eased closer to where Poops had run into the magical field. He could feel its vibration, and in the lowest registers of the dog's hearing, he could tell it was humming.

"I found one of the worm holes you told us about on the journey here," Gallarael grinned. "It isn't far." She paused as if she wasn't sure she should say what else was on her mind.

Vanx could tell.

"Spill it," he said, his voice full of agitation at being forced to ask.

"I think I know why the island has been divided." Gallarael started walking along the barrier, toward the building. "I think they are there to keep the things that live in each section from killing each other. I saw what roared. It was a gigantic pale furred spider-like thing. It didn't look happy that we are here, but it never sensed me." She put her hands out to the side, palms up. "I'm not sure what set it off."

"I hate spiders," Chelda said.

"Probably when Poops ran into the field and disturbed it," Anitha suggested. Vanx started to ask more questions but the look on Gal's face had turned severe. "What?"

"Get ready to fight," she warned before darting away, into the trees and out of sight.

"Vanx," came Chelda's voice. He could tell by her tone that something was behind them. "Bring it, Vanx."

Poops started barking and, for an instant, Vanx saw through the dog's eyes. There was a dozen or more of the larger tree-coons easing out of the woods in an attempt to hem them in. These had matted blood around their maws and what looked like vengeance in their eyes.

Vanx spun around. He didn't have to warn Moonsy or Anitha. They were already casting at the things.

The two elves, using spells, were able to destroy each creature they impacted with their magic, but the time to recast the spell allowed the things to get in too close.

Poops was just ahead of them, ready to pounce on one if it neared his companions. Vanx pulled himself out of his familiar's perspective, for Poops's angst and rage clouded his judgment.

Vanx knew he was about to have to get in the thick of them, for even more of the creatures were coming.

He sent a command out through the crystal that he doubted would help, but was worth the few seconds it took to do, just in case. Then he made sure to draw his family blade instead of the elven blade of healing.

Chelda was already pressing out away from the elves. Vanx saw her war hammer crunch into a coon-tail's skull, dropping it cold. She then sent another flailing through the air, off to the side.

Vanx took up position at the other side of the group and yelled at Chelda. "Stay out from in front of the elves."

"Yah," he heard her reply. "You'll stay out from in front of me, too, if you've any sense."

Chapter Eleven

> Ogres are full of menace,
> ogres are full of rage.
> Once a man was fool enough
> to put one in a cage.
> – a song from Dyntalla

Vanx's blade slid right into the first ring-tailed bastard that came at him. It was a head taller than he was, its head and maw a little larger than a dire wolf's, and he had a hard time feeling threatened by such a creature. The problem was, there were so many of them. This one fell away dead when he yanked his blade free. The next one, he skewered clawed him across the face. It didn't hurt, but blood came pouring into his eyes, blurring his vision.

One of the things hurled a rock that hit Moonsy right in the side of her head. The elven general fell over backwards, and Anitha and Poops both moved to protect her from the crazed creatures.

They must have smelled fresh blood for most of them started toward him or Moonsy. He had to duck a hurled stone and didn't quite get out of its way. He avoided a full impact, but his bell was rung, and he almost stumbled to his knees.

Poops leapt up and got a hold of the throat of one that came too close to Moonsy's fallen body, but the dog was slung away. To the pup's credit, he took a piece of flesh with him, leaving the creature confused and bleeding profusely. Some of the attackers stopped coming at them and started ripping the wounded coon apart, to feed.

A moment later, after seeing what would become of his friends if they were gotten a hold of, something burned through Vanx's blood. A murderous lust, like he'd felt fighting the Hoar Witch's evil horde. It carried him forward, right into the thick of them.

His boot found a furry chest, and he pushed off, turning a full backflip. As his feet went over his head, he sliced the neck of one, then another of the things. The growling, hissing creatures had a body more like a black bear's, than anything. He landed on both feet and had to immediately duck a swinging claw, but he pushed his blade up through that one's belly, under the ribs. He had to shoulder it over to its back to pull his blade free, and then he was spinning as he'd seen Zeezle do.

In moments, he had cleared an area around him. He glanced over and saw that, though Chelda was holding her own, Poops was now standing almost on top of Moonsy. Anitha was on her knees, holding her head as if she'd been cracked pretty good.

"Anitha," he yelled, drawing the Glaive of Gladiolus. He tossed her the elven sword, but wasn't sure she got it.

The sound of Chelda bashing and crunching the bastards was welcome, and the fact that she didn't even look to be winded yet was heartening. It was then that he saw twice as many of the things coming at them from the edge of the forest.

He looked and saw that Anitha hadn't grabbed the glaive, but instead had pitched forward. Poops was doing all a dog could do to stay on top of them, but Vanx knew that, even if he succumbed fully to his bloodlust and killed as many of these things as he could, this still wasn't going to end well.

A few of the creatures snatched their fallen and tore them apart, right there. They fed like they were starving, ripping open flesh and pulling it from the bone. Vanx decided there was no better motivation to survive than seeing what would happen to you if you missed a step. A glance at Poops and the elves showed him that Anitha was stirring, but one of the creatures had gotten hold of her ankle. It would have drug her into the bloody mess, but Poops sank his teeth into the creature's rib skin.

Vanx saw what was coming next and did something only his love for his dog would let him do.

The ringtailed, bear-bodied coon, brought its powerful fist down on Poops spine, and the dog yelped. Vanx had to force the dog from his mind again, even still he felt the severe pain the pooch was in.

Vanx took a great overhead swing and let go of his sword. He watched as it spun two full turns on its way to its target. When he was sure it was on its mark, he did a single cartwheel that landed with two feet on the ground, then two hands on the ground. From there, he launched, tucking and spinning right over the damned creature.

He landed with a foot on each side of his whining pup, but could do nothing for him just yet.

His sword had struck true. Before the thing fell, its chums were tearing it apart. Vanx saw the glaive and rolled toward it. When he came up holding it by the hilt, he stabbed Moonsy quickly, and then made to jab Anitha, but she was gone.

He poked Poops in the butt, and felt the wave of healing magic wash over his familiar.

His family sword was lost in the bloody mess now, and all he had was the glaive, a sword that healed instead of hurt.

Chelda was covered in splattered gore and still pounding and kicking anything that braved her proximity, and now that she saw Vanx had brought Moonsy back around she began to fight with more intensity, if that was possible.

"Save her." Moonsy pointed at where Anitha was being stretched by a creature holding her feet and another holding one of her arms.

Vanx didn't have anything to fight with, so he picked up one of the rocks that had been hurled at the elves and threw it right at the creature holding Anitha's feet. To his surprise, it dropped her when the stone hit. Poops darted out and leapt at the coon-tail still holding her arm, and sank his teeth into its furry wrist. Again, he was slung away, but another beast, a savage feline creature came bounding in, and not only clawed that confused thing deeply across the back, but then bounded to Poops's side and urged the dog back out of harm's way.

Vanx moved in and got ahold of the collar of Anitha's uniform.

Chelda was being driven back. Vanx saw that there were still twenty or more of the vicious cannibalistic things closing in, and a handful more were out there eating all the scraps.

"What do we do now?" Chelda called. "I can do this all afternoon, but not by—"

Chelda's words stopped as she tripped.

"Oh no," Moonsy croaked from the ground. She'd seen Chelda go down. Gallarael, in her fully shifted feline form, didn't hesitate. Vanx had to physically restrain Poops to keep him from joining them. Gallarael appeared right there in the mix with Chelda, but then blood started slinging away in all directions, and it was impossible to see if it was Chelda's, Gallarael's, or the mob of creatures crawling over the pile.

"Can you teleport us away or something?" Vanx asked Moonsy. He too was covered in blood, and it was his own, from the claw that had raked his forehead and brow.

"They're too far from us." The elven general looked at Vanx for answers.

Vanx had none. But even against the terrible odds he wasn't about to let his friend or his lover die. He ordered Poops to stay with Moonsy and charged into the mix without so much as a weapon.

Chapter Twelve

A dragon hunts its prey,
and roasts it with its fire.
Where does a dragon eat its meals?
Why anywhere it desires.
– Dragon's song

Vanx scanned the gore covered ground for his sword but didn't see it. He did stoop down and grab two rocks as he put his body in the pile of ring-tailed bastards his friends were under.

He felt claws tear into his legs, or maybe they were teeth. Then something, a heavy fist, he figured, pounded him in the ribs. He hit one of them with both rocks at the same time and it dropped to the ground, but he knew this was it. Before he could even turn to make another swing he was tackled, and then pounced on by three or more of them.

His arm was pulled and twisted, and he thought it was being ripped off, but then a screeching call resounded across the forest. Then another. He started to feel hope, but then a rock came down and hit him square in the face, leaving him in blackness.

*

When Vanx opened his eyes, he felt himself being drug across the ground. He raised his head to see Moonsy and Anitha, each with one of his legs in their hands.

"Poops," he sat up, looking for the dog.

Here, Poops responded in Vanx's mind. After a heartbeat of relief, his concern immediately went from his familiar to his love, and his friend. "Where are Gallarael and Chelda?"

"In the pile," Moonsy jabbed him with the Glaive of Gladiolus. "Now shake off the cobwebs and help." She barked the order as if he were a lowly sprite under her command.

Vanx complied and was glad someone had created a sense of order for him. His mind was scrambled, and he couldn't figure out what had happened to all of the things trying to kill them.

He saw Chelda, but Gallarael had been in changeling form, and was harder to pick out. Anitha found her, though, and Moonsy stuck Gallarael, and then Chelda with the glaive, and then dropped to her knees and recited an elven prayer for hope and life.

It didn't take long for both of them to stir.

Once concern over the ones he loved released its grip on his heart and mind, he asked Moonsy what happened.

"The great hawks came," Moonsy pointed to the two large predator birds. They were down the clearing feeding on coon tailed carcasses. They must have carried them away to eat undisturbed.

"How did they stop the attack?" Vanx saw so many dead tree-coons, he couldn't imagine how the birds had killed them all.

"They didn't stop it Vanx," Anitha said, as she helped roll one of the things off Gallaral's feline form.

"Then what happened to all of these turds." He pointed at all the dead creatures around them. His mind seemed to be swimming through a haze.

"You and Chelda killed most of them." Moonsy pulled her confused lover to a seated position and dropped to a knee to cleanse the disgusting, coppery blood from her face.

"Again, what happened?"

"The tree-coons fled when the birds came," Anitha said. "Your sword is over there." she pointed.

Vanx vaguely remembered, just before the battle ensued, that he'd grabbed the Hoar Witch's

55

crystal at his neck and screamed out for the great hawks. He hadn't known if they'd heard him or not.

Anitha was in his face then, Poops too. The elf seemed concerned about his forehead, and she used a dagger to do something that was really painful to his scalp.

"He will need the glaive again," Anitha said. She smiled a huge smile at Vanx. "Thank you, Master Vanx." She suddenly seemed like a shy child. "Thank you for saving me."

"And me," Chelda said.

"And me," Gallarael's voice brought his attention to her. She was in human form now, and had none of the blood and gore on her clothes that had been caked on her fur-like skin.

"I owe you, too, Vanx." Moonsy nodded. "I should have summoned the hawks. They suggested you used the witch's shard to call them in. That is what saved us all."

"There was no way he knew they'd scare the creatures away," Gallarael said, sitting opposite Anitha, over Vanx's body. "Don't let his ego swell too big."

"Ask Chelda." Vanx grinned, letting slip a half-felt bit of elation over having survived. "Those big birds, like the roc that attacked Anitha," Vanx looked at Chelda who nodded, and gave him a wink. She was covered in so much blood, her skin and clothes were stained crimson, save for her face. "They eat the coon-tailed bastards," Vanx continued. "We saw it happen when we were first here." He raised his upper body up to one elbow and looked at Chelda again. "Remember? Zeezle almost shit his pants. He was right under the tree Poops ran the damn coon-tail up."

"Those were the days." Chelda's voice dripped with sarcasm. "You should have kept that old man's map. It probably had more to it than you saw. Maybe not, though. He was a crazy farkin' son of a whore."

Vanx's heart stopped beating, but only as he decided that, even though Chelda was brash, and bold, and pretty much kept her musings to herself, she was as sharp as they come. The fact that she didn't talk a lot made it easy for people to think she wasn't paying attention, or was a dullard, or just a silly woman who cared little about anything.

But no, Vanx felt the rightness of what she'd just said, and knew in his heart that even Zeezle, had missed it, and Master Ruuk, too. And Ruuk was a Zythian wizard of great knowledge and skill.

Chelda was as smart as they come. It was just that simple. Her statement caused Vanx to remember that, when he'd possessed that map, he was able to see the island from the sea. They weren't able to see the island as they'd left it because Vanx had lost the map. Now he wondered what else they might see if they still had the obviously magicked parchment.

Vanx decided they needed the map before they proceeded. It was secured in a hopefully waterproof scroll-case. One the old wizard had bought him in Harthgar, and he had a good idea right where it was.

Chapter Thirteen

> No matter how many men venture in.
> No matter how hard they try.
> The Wildwood swallows everyone,
> who goes too far inside.
> – A song from Dyntalla

Since the two hawks were there, and neither Poops or Chelda could ride them, Vanx, Moonsy, and Anitha took the birds, Vanx on one, and the two elves on the other. This was after they'd spent most of the evening resting and full dark was on them.

None of them were overly concerned now. Everyone's full attention was on surviving. Anitha had warded them with every protection she knew, and the light spells from two powerful elves at once combined to make them seem like the sun flying through the sky.

Vanx could hardly see when the elves eased into his field of vision, but when they were behind him, the treetops, and the way the forest creatures fled them, was illuminated in vivid fashion.

This much light, in the bore-worm tunnel where he and Zeezle fought the thing with the tentacles, and the nasty pale crabs, would most likely ensure that nothing bothered this intrusion, but even with the protective wards and the light, the great hawks wouldn't fly them into the huge hole. Instead, the three were forced to wade into the fresh water to enter the ancient creature formed, rock-eater tunnel. Vanx decided he was glad he wasn't an elf, because the cold water was waist deep on them, where it only came up to his knees.

The Legend of Vanx Malic

Vanx was right about the oversized crabs. They fled like roaches scattering from the flare of a lantern. He hadn't counted on the strange four-legged, frog-skinned thing, that was apparently a nocturnal crab eater, though.

Anitha was fully prepared. Before Vanx could say a word, she took two steps forward and sent three lavender pulses at the toothy, frog-headed thing. They hit it in the hind end and, though they didn't do that much physical damage, the spell works exploded, bright and loud, when they impacted.

The thing leapt at them and Moonsy almost let a spell loose. Her decision to use restraint, was the right one, for it bounded right over them and went splashing to the shore startling the great hawks away.

"They'll return when I call them, Vanx. Come on." Moonsy must have seen him staring back, slack-jawed.

Vanx had seen something out in the lake. It was serpentine and huge and filled him with a fear like Pyra had.

"Cast a detection on the lake, Anitha," Vanx said, trying to master himself. "Let's get on with this."

"Uh," the eleven spell-caster stammered after the casting. "There must be a guardian creature in this section after all."

"I was hoping it was those coon-tailed bastards." Vanx used his head to indicate they should continue.

They started deeper into the borehole, and soon Vanx saw the passage leading up. Somewhere in the long windy passage was a creature that was probably still licking its wounds. It had been afraid of light, so Vanx wasn't concerned about it. He was concerned about the thing he'd seen in the lake, though. Especially since Anitha had let out a little gasp of surprise when she'd detected it with her spell.

"There is a way out of here, through a passage far too small for that that thing to—"

"It is a lake dragon," Anitha interjected. "A very old one."

"There is a passage leading out of here that the dragon cannot fit through," Vanx repeated. "I mean if it decides to pursue us. A short way inside the smaller cavern is where I think I lost the scroll case."

The lake dragon didn't follow them, but Vanx felt no less uneasy because of it. In fact, he remembered things about some dragons and started feeling a little guilt over mighty Pyra and Kelse's deaths. Those two dragons had given their lives to defeat the Paragon Dracus. The idea that this place was probably hidden so well, just to keep it away from that crazed blue bastard, made perfect sense, though, so he didn't dwell on the loss of his mighty winged friends that long.

They searched for a while, but it wasn't up in the beginings of the tunnel as Vanx had hoped.

"Is that it?" Moonsy asked, sloshing back into the lake from the gravel strewn beach formed by the tunnel's mouth.

It was. The map case was bobbing in the water, caught between two rocks that wouldn't let it float away.

"Yup," Vanx grinned. "Now which way do we go to get out of here?"

"Once we are in sight of the shore, I can teleport us there," Anitha said. "We can hide in the trees until the hawks come to General Moonseed's call."

"Okay," Vanx agreed. "But I don't want to end up being the lake dragon's dinner."

As soon as Moonsy handed the scroll case to him, Vanx checked to see if the map was still in the tube. It was, and it was dry.

The light seemed to keep everything away as they eased through the water trying to get around a bend so they could see the shore. Then they went, in a quick, unexpected flash, from standing in water, to standing in a swarm of gnats that were using the tree line to avoid the wind.

Not far away, the new jacaranda Heart Tree had grown so tall that it dominated the night. The moon was almost full, and somehow the tree had found a way to hide most of it.

Vanx let out a sigh of relief. He wanted to see the passage under the magical wall, Gallarael had found.

"Here they come," he heard Anitha say.

One of the great hawks flapped down between the trees and the water's edge. The other was illuminated brightly in the eleven light as it glided toward them. The water exploded under the bird and a sleek, dragonly head shot up, its toothy maw opened wide enough to take the whole bird with a single bite.

Vanx's heart exploded, and he heard both of the elves scream, but there was little else any of them could do.

Chapter Fourteen

> The dragon belched his fire,
> and the knight he did a dance.
> It was for naught, the fire was hot,
> and he didn't stand a chance.
> – Dragon's Song

"What's on the other side of the— the magic wall thing?" Chelda asked. They had a huge fire going, and she and Gallarael had their backs almost against the strange structure. They were on each side of Sir Poopsalot, giving him absentminded attention.

They'd decided that neither of them needed to sleep until Vanx and Moonsy returned. There was so many dead tree-coons, though, that Gallarael figured anything looking for a meal could find one in the shadows instead of bothering them.

"About the same, only there is an entryway into the building around the corner and down the other face of it," Gallarael answered. "I mean there is an alcove, and in it, a few steps leading up to some doors, but they looked locked." She harrumphed, trying to find the right words. "I couldn't check them because I— I was—"

"I get it," Chelda saved her the struggle. "You had paws, not hands. That changeling stuff almost got your head cracked the other day when you came out of the woods." She paused for a bit. "They are probably locked," Chelda eventually continued. "Maybe we should go see? It would be safer for us inside."

"Safer?" Gallarael laughed. "When has Chelda Flar been concerned with safer? You just want to go see."

"Am I that easy to read?"

"When you start talking about caution, you are."

"Either way, I want to go look." Chelda snorted. "How's that for caution."

"What do you think, pup?" Gallarael asked the dog. Poops gave a yip that Vanx might have been able to decipher, but the way his tail wagged it was clear he would do whatever they wanted to do.

"I think he agrees," Chelda offered. She got to her feet. "Come on."

"Chelda," Gallarael felt like a mom scolding a child. "We will go, but in the morning, with or without Vanx. Just wait until there is some daylight. There is no telling what sort of creatures are over there."

"Yah," the eager gargan sat back down. "I suppose daylight would be better." She seemed disappointed, but only until Gallarael asked her about Harthgar and the final battle with the Paragon Dracus. Gallarael wanted to know all about how Vanx acted when he'd thought her dead. And Chelda, once she started bragging about the exploits of Zeezle and Vanx, held nothing back.

Then, from the far side of the ridge, the sky was lit up in dramatic fashion. The roaring sound that erupted with the luminary display wasn't the same sort of roar they'd heard earlier, but it was no less powerful.

The brightness and feel of the concussion that followed hit them hard enough to make Poops get behind Gallarael and whimper.

*

Anitha's protective wards were far more potent than anyone expected. When the lake dragon's maw closed over the warded great hawk, an explosion of sorts ruined its meal.

The moonlit area was suddenly illuminated with stark magical light, and the sound of crackling static scorching the unsuspecting water wyrm's mouth sent chills through Vanx's bones.

As fast as it had grabbed the hawk, the lake dragon opened its mouth, or rather, its mouth was forced back open by Anitha's powerful magic. The little elven spell caster wasn't done, either. She was already letting loose a hot, sizzling pulse, which streaked at the lake dragon's middle section, from her outstretched hand.

When it connected with the surprised amphibian, the creature emitted a roar that held as much pain as it did anger, but it was loud enough to hurt Vanx's ears nonetheless.

The lake dragon turned to gaze at them then. It paused long enough to get a good look, and then it dove.

The great hawk wasn't out of danger just yet, however. The power of the wyrm's jaws had broken a wing, and the stunned bird spun around, once twice, and then, as the magical light faded, it spun around again and crashed into the trees a few hundred paces from where they stood.

"Do you think it is gone?" Vanx asked.

"I think it is in so much pain that it won't try us again this night," Moonsy said nodding. "Good work." She patted Anitha on the shoulder and urged them all into a sprint.

Vanx took the Glaive of Gladiolus up into the tree and stuck the bird with it. The hawk was terrified at first, but it relished the feel of the magic. It stretched its wings, and Vanx heard the frail bones popping back into place. He thought he could hear them knitting together. Then the bird started flapping madly to pull itself free from the branch that had impaled its body.

Vanx stabbed the bird with glaive again, and when it tried to fly away this time, the limb came loose in a wet sounding slurp. Vanx half-climbed, half-jumped down from the tree.

He saw the hawk land near the elves, and Vanx followed them up the slope away from the water's edge to where the other hawk was hiding.

"That was too close," Moonsy said.

"Yup," Vanx nodded. "I thought we lost the bird."

"We may have," Anitha said, matter of factly. "It is still riding the rush of fear, and all that magic, but after those sensations subside, the healed wing may not support a rider."

"Then we better get back to the others quickly." Moonsy indicated she and Anitha would be riding the previously wounded hawk.

Vanx mounted the other one and, a moment later, they were above the trees, save the tip-top of the Heart Tree's upper limbs.

The sun had already started to pinken the distant horizon. After the battle with the tree-coons and the lake dragon, Vanx knew there would be no sleeping. He had to rest his eyes though, and his mind, while he could.

He wasn't that tired, but he was anxious. He was also curious about what Gallarael had found on the other side of the magical barrier.

Chapter Fifteen

> In her father's barn,
> she took my coins again.
> But oh what Molly gave me,
> I'll remember 'till my end.
> – Parydon Cobbles

As they flew, Vanx closed his eyes and sought a state of reverie, hoping the short rest would be enough to keep him sharp through the coming day. He never found true slumber, but he did allow his orbs to vanquish the bright splotches Anitha's magic had bright burned into them.

When they landed, all the light showed him just how many carrion critters were having a feast. Small red eyed, animals and insects, eight-legged, four-legged, and two, fled the brightness of the illumination spells.

It seemed like he had just shut his lids. He didn't complain, for here came Poops, braving the birds, who instinctually stirred fear deep inside him. The dog was waggling from side to side, like a four-legged fish trying to swim through the air. Vanx slid from the great hawk and greeted his friend from a squatted position.

"Ya, find it?" Chelda asked.

"We did," Moonsy answered with a forced smile. "Nearly lost one of the hawks to a water wyrm, though."

"There is a dragon here?" Gallarael asked. Even after the light spells were extinguished, Vanx could see her nervousness.

Vanx remembered seeing her crushed in the maw of a terrible wyrm of sorts. Her thickened shapeshifter skin had saved her from the sharp puncturing teeth, but not from the compression of that bastard's bite. It didn't kill her, but had killed their child.

He left Poops to give her a reassuring hug.

"It was a lake dragon, love" he said softly. "It won't stray too far from its domain."

"And Anitha blistered its mouth raw." Moonsy was clearly proud of the other elf. "Her wards protected the great hawk when the lake dragonb tried to eat it."

"I'm ready to go to the other side and see what is waiting," Chelda said, indicating her backpack was loaded and she was waiting. "Gal said there was a door over there."

"A door?" Vanx looked at Gallarael. "Why didn't you say anything?"

"I would have, but you were intent on getting the map before proceeding." Gallarael put her hands on her hips and smirked. "You said that once you had it, you might be able to see more than you can with your eyes."

He *had* said that.

Vanx pulled the scroll case from his belt and popped off the oiled leather cap. "It was floating in the rocks at the edge of the lake," he said as he unrolled the parchment. "I can't believe it's still dry."

Vanx looked at the old wizard's map for a moment. "Where is Papri's map?" he asked.

He glanced around at the gray-blue, cloud-filled morning, and decided he needed help to see. "Moonsy, can you give me a little bit of light, please."

Before she could cast her spell, he turned and gave her a serious look. "A little light, general," he grinned. "Like a candle, not like a bonfire."

Moonsy nodded and a small orb of illumination appeared. She sent it to hover over Vanx's head with a subtle gesture of her hand. Vanx avoided looking at the orb. Instead, he concentrated on the maps, or more precisely the differences he saw in them.

"Look at that," Chelda said from over his shoulder. "The crazy one marked the magic wall things, too."

"Moonsy, what is this word?" Vanx asked. "Anitha, you're the eldest here, have you any idea what this language is? What this word means?"

"It's probably the name of the map maker, Vanx."

"Nah, nah," he shook his head. "That old wizard drew this, I'm sure of it. I don't think that is his mark at all. But I am starting to think he may have had something to do with creating this place."

"This is a natural island, Vanx," Moonsy said. "He may have made it invisible, but he didn't create it."

"Maybe the trickster did?" Vanx wondered aloud.

"Who is the trickster?" Chelda asked.

"The old man mentioned him. He was the father of my race, maybe?" Vanx shrugged. "But he made a simple old cave look like it was an ancient dwarven complex. The pitfalls were ridiculous."

"The place you had to piss in a hole to get out of?" Chelda blurted out a laugh. "I thought you made that up? You can tell the story as we hike, man." Chelda's impatience was showing. "The day has begun, and we are still dallying and guessing. What we want is below us, and behind closed doors we haven't even seen yet."

"You're right, Chel." Vanx put away the map. He hadn't noticed anything that would help them. Only the word on the bottom of the parchment stood out. He looked and saw that all of their gear was stowed. They were all ready to follow Gallarael to the other side and were waiting on him.

The smell of the dead tree-coons was strong, especially to Poops's nose, and flies covered most of them like an undulating carpet. There were several bright blue-fleshed sea dactyls feasting on the ripe corpses. There were other birds, too, but they gave the ancient dactyls all the space they wanted. Vanx even saw a few of the small red marked spiders dragging pieces of meat into the woods.

Poops barked at something that braved their immediate proximity and, not for the first time, Vanx wished he'd brought a bow along. He was hungry and the rations he'd had in his belt pack had gotten wet sloshing through the lake.

"Here." Chelda must have seen him tossing soggy pieces of sea biscuit and jerked venison out as they went along. The piece of meat she gave him wasn't jerked or even cooked. She gave him a curious look when he looked from the thick morsel to her face and back.

Chelda had a little blood on her lips.

"Is this meat from those things we killed?" Vanx asked. "Unfired?"

"Yah." Chelda grinned as she took a bite and had to pull the meat away hard to tear it from the rest.

Vanx shook his head, but took a bite anyway. It was pretty good, but tough. After tearing a second chunk off with his teeth, he gave the rest to Poops, who sniffed it three times before chugging it down, half chewed.

They soon entered a small bore-worm hole. The almost perfectly formed circular tube was just big around enough that Chelda didn't have to stoop to go in.

Ten paces later, they could all see a circle of light in the distance.

"There." Gallarael seemed excited. "A short sprint to the right will take us to the alcove I saw."

Chapter Sixteen

> We're off to go a questing,
> a questing we will go.
> What we find and who'll survive,
> we'll find out when we know.
> - A Tavern Song

Just before she exited the borehole, Gallarael dropped low and shushed them. "Something is out there," she whispered. "Maybe we should wait until it leaves."

"Maybe I could go bash its skull." Chelda's voice wasn't restrained at all.

"Shhh," Vanx heard Moonsy try to quiet her lover.

A few moments passed.

"It's all right," Gallarael looked back. "Whatever it was, Chel's voice startled it away."

"You didn't see it?" Vanx asked.

"No," she looked back at Vanx and met his eyes. "Sensed more like. It was big enough to make the lower branches shake, though. Maybe it left some tracks."

"I'd rather avoid these things around here than investigate them," said Anitha, glancing at her general defiantly, as if voicing her opinion might be out of line.

"Yup. I agree," Vanx said before Moonsy could react. "Lead us to the doorway you told Chelda about. I want to see it for myself."

"If it ain't locked, it's a trap," Chelda said.

"This whole place seems like an elaborate trap," Moonsy agreed.

"Yup," added Vanx. "But we're not getting caught in it."

"You don't sound as sure as you think you do," Gallarael told him.

"Go." Chelda urged Gallarael out of the opening. "Let's get on with it."

"Let's." Vanx let all the women exit before him, and then followed Poops, who darted up to the font of the single file procession. Vanx let his senses meld with the dogs, and the world took on a whole other level of definition. He could detect the heat of things as he took them in, and he could sharpen his vision a bit, but the brilliant scentscape that opened up was what always astounded him the most.

He could smell the acrid insects, and the sweet nectar of some honeysuckle that grew in a sizable cluster not-so-far away. There was a snake flicking its tongue on a high branch, and a small finch showing anger with a shrill, three-note warning whistle. Vanx could smell the women ahead of him and distinguish each one's individual scent. He could also smell himself, and decided that he should have bathed in the lake, or at least splashed water on his pits.

He was ripe.

Vanx could smell the slippery scent of a lizard lazing in a ray of sunlight a few trees away, and he could feel, as well as smell, the vibrations of fear coming from more than one hunkering little hopper. The flowers and the different vegetation were distinguishable as well. He almost laughed when he had a thought.

If he failed at adventuring, he could always make a fancy pocketful of coins seeking out herbs with Poops's keen snout.

He laughed at himself again, for he had Pyra's hoard, and a pair of leviathan to protect it. By the hells, if he added one more ship he would officially have a fleet. If he weren't committed to the Goddess, he'd be fishing somewhere this very moment.

Follow your heart, she always told him.

His heart told him to finish what he started, and then enjoy all that came his way, when it was done, but he was a bard. He'd sang many a song about one who waited to *follow their heart,* and then missed the ship, so-to-speak. He would do the bidding of the one who had allowed him this life, but he would be quick about it. Or so he hoped.

Vanx was lead to the corner of the building. It wasn't that large, he decided, and it wasn't square as poor Papri had drawn it. It was long and fairly narrow, and from one vantage, when they'd gone uphill to avoid a fallen tree, he saw that is was flat, or maybe canted so slightly as to be imperceptible to the eye.

They were about half way from the corner to the centered alcove, along the longer side, when Vanx stopped them.

"Anitha, can you levitate straight up from here and tell me what the top of this place really looks like?"

"I can," she nodded and prepared to do so.

"What is it Vanx?" Moonsy asked. He looked up to see three women, each with nearly the same hand-on-their-hip look, as if he was keeping them from a gala, or a festival dance.

"From the ridge, we just saw the corner, is all. The top is lower than the trees." He shrugged. "When we went up to avoid that fallen trunk, I thought I saw that part of it was darker than the rest."

Birds? Poops sent the cautionary suggestion to Vanx through their familiar link.

"Watch out for birds, Anitha," Vanx said quickly as the small elf rose.

"You have to be kidding," Anitha said, shaking her head.

She didn't have to go very high to start excitedly describing something. "It's a dragon."

"What?" Chelda asked. Vanx noticed her heavy war hammer was already in her hand.

"Not a real dragon, but a long snaking dragon shape, done in darker stone than the rest. It has its wings pulled back, save for a darker, rectangular border."

"I wonder if there are more dragons here," Gallarael said. "This island could host several of them."

"Another Castovanti," Chelda barked out in a laugh.

Vanx laughed, too. Not at Chelda's remark, but the way Moonsy looked up at her with a wide opened mouth.

Then a roar sounded, causing Vanx to drop into a ready position. The sun was shaded from overhead for so long that he thought his heart might burst out of his chest.

"To the alcove," Vanx yelled, and started running. He nearly ran into Moonsy, who was standing there with tears streaming down her elfish face. His heart clenched in his chest as he realized Anitha had just been snatched from where she was hovering, by a dragon. A dragon who most likely used this building's top as a lazing stone.

Chapter Seventeen

> There are many ways to skin a cat,
> the fun is choosing which.
> But it's no cat I want to kill.
> I want to skin a witch."
> – The Weary Wizard

Vanx forced Moonsy to go ahead of him and, when he entered the alcove, he looked out and saw that the dragon was only half as big as Pyra had been, which was still pretty large as far as dragons go. It was the color of a coral sea, or maybe a light, turquoise stone. And it was circling back around.

Looking at what was outside the small cube of space they were huddled in, Vanx saw that there was plenty of room for the wyrm to fly by and blast them with whatever sort of breath a coral blue dragon might produce. Vanx had no idea such a beautiful creature existed. There was no dragon lore he knew of that catalogued a wyrm of such a color. When it banked, he saw a coppery colored pattern ran down its spine. He could imagine it still along a seashore looking like a tumble of stones at the water's edge. There was no way he could guess what it could do.

"They are locked," Chelda said loudly.

"Let me see," Moonsy stepped up. At first she looked like she was in shock over losing Anitha so abruptly. She shook it off, and went about studying the handle and latch on the heavy banded wood filling the arch.

Poops barked, sending a shock of warning and fear down Vanx's spine. He turned again to see that the dragon was coming at them now. His heart was hammering, and he was almost certain they were about to die, but something compelled him.

Everything suddenly made sense.

"By the Lanch and Lecher, he's gone mad," Chelda said when Vanx started out toward the dragon.

"There's no keyhole, Vanxy." Moonsy sounded frantic. "There isn't a keyhole!" She yelled it this time, probably thinking he didn't hear. He'd remembered what the old wizard had said about dragons, and he hoped beyond all hope that he was right, assuming that he now understood what the word written in the corner of that map was.

"Havoktalla!" Vanx yelled at the approaching wyrm. "We mean you no harm. Havoktalla!" He repeated the dragon's name a second time.

"The door opened, Vanx!" Moonsy squealed.

"Come on Vanx," Gallarael yelled. "The door opened."

"Hurry," Chelda echoed their plea.

Vanx didn't understand.

Poops blasted through his brain with painfully dire barks.

Vanx shook off his delusion and fear overtook him. He turned and started to run back toward them. He took two steps but his legs turned to water when he sensed the dragon about to snatch him from the ground.

His face banged into the dirt so hard it bounced up. Shadow blocked the daylight, and the wind from wide scaly wings blew grass and debris in his eyes. But when his face came back down, hard, cold stone greeted his cheek.

"That was farkin' close, yah." Chelda hefted him to his feet. Vanx had to hold onto the gargan while his heart slowed its thumping.

Moonsy must have teleported him out of harm's way.

"It's coming!" Gallarael warned.

Vanx couldn't believe he'd thought the word was the dragon's name, or that by invoking it, he might befriend the creature. Pyra had warned him that few wyrms had a concern for humanity. And no one ever said anything about how much a person would long for the companionship of a mighty dragon after befriending, and then losing, such a wholly awesome friend, either.

Even worse, Vanx couldn't wrap his mind around the idea that he had just asked Anitha to raise up to her death.

She was gone.

Not even the Glaive of Gladiolus would bring her back.

Havoktalla was just a password, or keyword, that unlocked the doors leading into the dragon's lazing stone. The moment he thought the word, though, the doors slammed shut, and bolted tight behind them.

It happened so suddenly that it almost took Chelda's arm off.

They dragon was right there about to blast them with its breath, and then they were apparently locked inside.

Flames leapt to life, on the tips of torches ensconced evenly along each wall. The light revealed that there were three doors on each side of the wide fancily tiled vestibule.

A grand, carved-stone staircase circled down in about what Vanx thought was the middle of the structure. Beyond that, he could see there was a pew lined great hall. The fancy banded double door that opened up into it was open, and by the look of the tarnish on the metal, and the amount of dust accumulated on the banisters, the air in here hadn't been disturbed in more than a decade.

Oddly, Poops conveyed that it reminded him of the ancient building under the black spire in Harthgar. Vanx thought this might be because it was formed of the same type of stone, or more likely to the dog, it smelled the same.

"I can cast a detection similar to the ones Anni used." Moonsy fought to contain her sadness. "Hers were stronger and more accurate, though."

"It's all right, love," Chelda said soothingly. She started to put her hand on her elven lover's shoulder, but to everyone's surprise, Moonsy shrugged it off.

"NO! No, it is not all right, *love*," Moonsy shouted. The last word was bathed in venomous sarcasm. Chelda recoiled, a stricken look on her face. "I've known Anitha longer than you and Vanx have been alive combined." She started to tremble, but Gallarael went to her. "How would you feel if you just lost a friend so dear."

Chapter Eighteen

> I told her that her eyes,
> were bluer than the sky,
> Then she picked my pockets,
> as she gave a kiss goodbye.
> – Parydon Cobbles

It took her a few moments, but Moonsy eventually gathered herself. She didn't so much as glance Chelda's way, and Chelda just stared at the doors opening on the great hall, looking at something far beyond what was before her.

Vanx knew them all too well. He hadn't spent as much time with Moonsy as the other two, but he and Chelda had been at sea together for months at a time, and they eventually shared everything, so he knew a lot more about General Gloryvine Moonseed than maybe she thought he did. He also knew Chelda was hurt right now.

Instead of consoling Chelda, as Gallarael was Moonsy, Vanx eased over to the gargan woman and shouldered her to get her attention.

"General Moonseed, when you can cast your detection spell, please do. Chelda and I will go explore the great hall."

"I'll stay with her." Gallarael gave Vanx a tight lipped smile.

Vanx started to urge Poops to come with he and Chelda, but the dog had gone to Moonsy and was licking her face, forcing smiles out of her grief.

The great hall was just as dusty and unused as the entry and stairwell had been. "We should just go down," Chelda said. "I'm in a mood to bash something now."

"You're always in a mood to bash something, Chel," Vanx joked. "And the elves, as old and smart as they are, are not usually bold adventurers, like we are. Losing you, Poops, or Gal, even Zeezle, would make me crumble. Moonsy just needs time to get over the loss of Anitha."

"They were lovers once," Chelda said, shocking Vanx with the amount of understanding conveyed in the words. "When they were younger, they had a thing." She turned to Vanx and shrugged. "She'll not easily get over it."

"Maybe not," he pointed at the scene depicted on a tapestry hanging behind the podium at the far end of the room, and moved that way. "But she will get over it, just as she got over the loss of her uncle."

"Gah," Chelda turned him by the shoulder from behind. She looked down at him studying his eyes. "You can't even say his name, can you?"

Vanx shrugged again and went to look at the tapestry.

"I'm adventuring with a bunch of doll hugging sentimentalists.," She barked out a laugh. "I can only hope to die as well as Foxwise Posey-Thorn did. Thorn died a warriors death."

"We love you, too, Chel." Vanx chuckled at her, but it was a grim laugh for Anitha's death was on his shoulders, or at least he felt that way. "Just stop and try and imagine how you would feel if me or Poops died."

"But you'd never die," she said. "I won't let you."

"While that is a comforting notion," he gave her a glance. "You know it could happen. Think about it for a moment."

Vanx then focused on the tapestry. There was a wonderful castle in the background with golden spires that managed to shine through the gloom of the rest of the captured moment. There was a lake before the castle. In the lake there was a huge, dark monster sending plumes of purple smoke into the air. Around it, the sky was filled with colorful dragons, some with riders, some not. They were fighting demons of every sort, while on the ground a full-on war between man and fiend raged.

It was an awesome battle, and he'd sung about it a few hundred times, but mainly in one long tune, called the *Ballad of Ornspike*.

The idea that the humans and dragons had won was a testament to the will of men. Learning what he had from the old wizard, about how some dragon spelled "trickster" mage, and a high elf had mated to create his whole race was a little farfetched, and went against all of his history lessons, but he and Zeezle had always thought there was a deeper truth being kept from them as they were growing up.

He couldn't say if it was true or not, but the old wizard and his Goddess seemed to be urging him in the same direction. Who was he to disbelieve? It didn't matter now. Zythians were here, a hearty race that would never give up their small continent.

"Look at those spiders." Chelda's voice wasn't as sure as it had been earlier.

Vanx saw she was looking at a tightly woven web in the corner of the room. There were a handful of fingertip-sized arachnids, each of them had a bright white jag on its main section.

"Those aren't the kind that bit Zeezle," Vanx said. "That one was a baby version of the big scarlet marked bastards that we had to fight to go down the hole. It was the size of a gourd melon."

"I remember," Chelda said. "And I tried what you suggested, but I couldn't for the life of me find a way to imagine my life without you and Sir Poopsalot in it."

"I'm sure Moonsy felt the same sort of thing about Anitha, before— before—"

"Yah," Chelda answered. "I'll talk to her when she is done doing her sorcery."

Chapter Nineteen

> They came on clever ships of wood,
> those that called themselves men.
> They spread like mice through fertile fields,
> and overtook the land.
> – Balladamned (a Zythian song)

"Come!" Gallarael's voice echoed through the great hall from where she'd poked her head in the doorway. "Moonsy has finished."

Vanx followed Chelda to where the elf was squatted by the stairwell. She was spoiling Poops with attention.

"I suppose the thing radiating all the magic is what we are after?" Moonsy looked at Vanx questioningly.

"I can't say what we are after," Vanx answered truthfully. "All I know is that here, on this island somewhere, is something that is supposed to lead us to the remaining gems and hopefully let us know where to smash them, too."

"We are not necessarily looking for something magical, then." Moonsy sighed. "But something as powerful as what I am detecting cannot be ignored."

"Something showing such power is probably just bait for a trap," Chelda said.

Vanx could tell his gargan friend wasn't happy. She'd been in a mood since Moonsy had snarled at her. Or maybe the attitude stemmed from Gallarael comforting Moonsy after Chelda's brash remarks earlier? Vanx decided not to think about it anymore. There was no sense worrying over what women were going to do, for they were going to do it no matter what.

"Probably is a trap," Gallarael agreed. She looked to Vanx to be thinking about something, probably Anitha, but maybe about their current situation? He couldn't guess. "Dragons don't get spelled to guard over prizes that are not powerful, or at least valuable," she finished.

"You think the dragon is spelled?" Vanx asked Gallarael.

"I do," she replied, nodding. "It has to be. Why else would it care about us? I mean, if it weren't bound here, it would have a hoard and lair, not a fancy lazing stone, or whatever you called it." She looked at Vanx for support.

"It might have just come upon this island." Chelda gave Gallarael a look that showed she wasn't pleased. "Who says it doesn't have a lair. And it might have been after us because it was simply hungry. Here, it has a protected, invisible island. A sea-locked platter full of giant four-legged frog beasts and tree-coons to feed on. It is king— or queen— here. It would stay for those reasons alone."

"It is likely just drawn to the magic below us, or it could be spelled to it." Moonsy swallowed back tears. "Anitha told me, after casting her detections, that she thought whatever was down there," Moonsy pointed at the stairwell, "would be heavily warded and have traps, and guardians to negotiate before we could even get to it to see what it was." She then pointed up. "A dragon guarding the entrance to this place suggests she was correct." She looked at Chelda, then added, "If it is guarding this place at all."

Chelda nodded, and started down the stairs with her war hammer at the ready. She didn't stop when no one else immediately came with her.

The others did follow, first Moonsy, then Gallarael and Poops, leaving Vanx to bring up the rear. He drew his old blade and was irked that it still had some tree-coon gore stuck to the steel near the hilt. As they descended the similarly torch-lit circular staircase,

Vanx used the glaive's tip to chip the hardened bits of furred flesh off his family sword. Then he put the glaive back in its sheath and used a wad of spit, and the hem of his filthy shirt to rub away the bits that remained.

"It will have to do," he mused aloud, looking at the smooth metal. In the reflection, he saw how dirty and haggard he looked. He didn't feel bad physically, but he hurt for Moonsy's loss, and felt more guilt over Anitha's death than he should have. Or maybe he didn't feel as much as he should. All he knew was that he was glad it wasn't Gal, Chelda, or Poops that the dragon had snatched. If it was, he'd be far worse off than Moonsy was now. Which was a testament to all she'd been through recently.

"Should we have checked those doors by the entry?" Gallarael asked. She stopped at the first of many landings. These wider treads caused the actual shape of the stairwell to be oval, not round. Every other one of them had an archway, the ones without openings, were plain flat sections. All of them, at least for the first few levels down, had a flickering torch ensconced on the wall. Eventually, Vanx figured, there could be an opening on both sides farther down.

The archways led to a floor, which meant that each level could have a ceiling fifteen feet high, or more. The stone steps continued down, on and on, into darkness, and that in itself was unnerving. "What if what we are really after, was just right there? Those rooms had to be sizable, and for whoever maintained this place, they would be the most practical to use."

"You are fierce fiend in battle, Princess," Chelda laughed from below. "And you did more than your share against the Hoar Witch, and that flat-headed farkin' blue thing when we were at war, but adventuring is what me and Vanx do." She stopped and made eye contact with Vanx and Gallarael, in turn. "It's never that easy." She looked certain. "Is it Vanx? It is never that easy."

"It never is, Chel." Vanx had to agree, but what Gallarael said made perfect sense. The best way to hide something here would be to leave it in the open and distract whoever would be looking, toward something else.

"Hold up," Vanx called. Chelda was already standing on the second landing. This one, as expected, opened up on another torchlit expanse of stone floor. Poops was a few steps below her, wondering if he should continue down or stay at the second level. "We should go back up and check the rooms so it is done," Vanx said. "Gallarael has a point."

"Bah!" Chelda laughed. "I suppose it is better to check them now than listen to you wonder about it the rest of the way." Moonsy had just joined her on the landing, but Chelda stepped back on the stairs and started up.

Corresponding exactly with the first step she took, Vanx heard a sound, through Poops's keen ears. It was mechanical noise, like a stronghold's gate latch being ratcheted closed. Poops leapt completely from the stairs to Moonsy's side on the landing, forcing them both to roll into the room beyond. With Chelda's second step came a surprise that sent Vanx's heart into his throat and made his stomach feel like it was filled with flies.

The landing tilted. The treads and risers, folded underneath their boots, or unfolded really. It happened so fast that he was sliding before he figured out what was going on. Now he, Gallarael, and Chelda were rolling and tumbling around and down the spiraling ramp back under and out of sight from Moonsy and Poops.

Vanx had to struggle to keep the glaive and his family blade from getting tangled with his legs, as he went. When he bounced off of the thing Gallarael had changed into, he almost lost control of them and impaled himself. Luckily, the swords were sheathed and he was paying attention.

Gallarael had elongated her fingers and dug them into the stone, causing chips and flakes of rock, as well as sparks, to mar the surface. Then her claw tips found a seam and she stopped. Vanx didn't try to grab on because he was repulsed. Instead, he maintained his concentration on not breaking a leg, a sword, or his skull, as he and Chelda continued to tumble into the darkness.

The dark, hard-skinned, humanoid creature Gallarael was now, reminded him of crossing the Frozen Falls. Her shapeshifting hadn't been as practiced then, but it hadn't bothered him either. It was because, back then, they hadn't been lovers, he decided.

His lapse in concentration was rewarded when his head cracked into the wall and stars filled his eyes. After that, he was too dizzy to do more than keep the blades pressed against his legs.

Chapter Twenty

> Old Master Wiggins,
> he loved the Spring Fair jig.
> He twirled and spun so hard and fast,
> he lost his silly wig.
> – a Parydon street ditty

Vanx had to shake his head to clear the dizziness from it, but he already knew what the stuff sticking to his skin was. This knowledge was enough to have his heart pounding because there was nothing else like the feel of spider webs against you.

"Chelda," he called in a semi-quiet hiss. "Chelda are you all right?"

"Yah," she responded, sounding a little bewildered. "This stuff is— is—"

"Stay still! Stay still and close your eyes," Vanx said. He waited a moment and made sure to recite the words to the Hoar Witch's spell correctly. It was a spell from a section of her old book where she'd written down the ways she dealt with the monsters she created. This one was for Sissy and her webs. He didn't open his eyes when the workings sent a quick powerful blast of flame out from his hand, but he wanted to.

He was falling then, and he heard Chelda thump into something just as the wind was knocked from his lungs. He passed out of consciousness but, before he did, he saw the dense spread of spider webs above them. Some of the dangling ends floated around crazily, the flames from his magic slowly consuming them in a sparkling blue flame. Some weren't affected at all and, as the blackness swallowed him, he saw one of the red glowing spiders. This one was as big as the

Ada Rosamond. It was covered in tiny little spiders, just like the one that almost killed Zeezle, only smaller.

It was having a little trouble negotiating the many webs made by the lesser arachnoids, but still Vanx's heart was frozen with fear.

Vanx opened his eyes to a splash of cool water and Chelda's concerned expression. He was disappointed to see that the spider he'd seen wasn't a dream. It was still coming, and what he'd thought was its inability to get around the spinnings of lesser spiders, was just its motherly caution.

Chelda hadn't noticed it yet, which was for the best. Vanx knew she was terrified of any sort of arachnoid. Vanx closed his eyes after smiling at her and did something he rarely did. He cast a spell intending to kill something. The fact that it had so many baby spiders attached to it weighed on his conscience, but the instinct to survive overrode his guilt.

His pupils must have focused for Chelda started to turn to see what was looming down at them. Vanx used his left hand to grab her hair and keep her from seeing. His right hand pointed up at the thing just as its needle sharp spinneret came out. A single drop of the terrible stuff in it dripped and landed on Chelda's back. Vanx saw that it was a strand of web and that it was about to yank Chelda away from him.

Vanx blasted the spider into an up-spray of disintegrated mush with a kinetic pulse that cleared the webs for as far up as he could see. It also coated the walls of the vertical boreworm tunnel with the red glowing stuff that particular strain of arachnoids produced.

"Turn round," Vanx said, snatching the canteen Chelda was holding. He washed the webbing from her.

"What in all the hells was that, Vanx?" she asked.

"A bat," he lied. "It's gone now."

Chelda looked up and saw all the glowing crimson splatter. Then she turned back to Vanx. "Thank you."

"I wasn't just saving your hide, Chel." Vanx let her pull him to his feet. "I was saving my own arse, too."

"I meant for the lie," she shook her head. "I fought those spiders with you, Zeezle, and the sea mage by the old wizard's hole, remember? There is no mistaking that glow, or that smell."

"We were just talking about it. That's why I lied." He patted her on the shoulder. "Are you all right? No bones need mending with the glaive?"

"Nah." She smirked at him, and he saw the girlishness in the look.

The eerie red glow gave everything a sinister tint, but Vanx used the illumination to take it all in.

There was man sized arch leading away from the smooth floored, but otherwise unnatural looking cavern. If this was a boreworm hole, the thing dug down to here and just stopped. The only irregularities in the otherwise flat bottom were formed from rock falls. If it was a borehole, it was old enough that the effects of the creature's secretion had worn off.

The rock eaters left a substance that stopped stalags from forming in horizontal tunnels and strengthened the almost smooth sides they left as they chewed through the world, he guessed so that they could use the tunnels again unhindered. Vanx walked toward the archway, and Chelda followed. He took a moment to reach out to Poops through their familiar link, but he couldn't sense anything.

He wasn't alarmed, for they'd tumbled down that circular ramp for a long time. It was a long way back to the top, and he figured there was magic involved. He'd seen Poops and Moonsy as safe as could be on the second level of the structure, and Gallarael, was near the third level, if she hadn't found a way to climb back up to the others.

Vanx cast a simple detection spell, and was surprised to feel the radiant power of something not too far into the opening he'd just spotted.

"Come," he said.

*

When Gallarael, in one of her partially shifted forms, came scratching her way up the ramp, Poops barked at her. Moonsy had to hug the agitated dog to keep him from getting on the tilted treads, but he let her restrain him.

Gallarael finally made it to the floor and changed into her most human form. She dropped to soothe Poops immediately but gave Moonsy a dire look.

"What?" Moonsy asked.

"I went down before I came back up," Gallarael spoke as she rubbed the dog's gruff.

"They went tumbling into a dark cavern and I didn't see them after that." Gallarael stood. "They have the glaive so if they survived the landing they should be all right."

"What do we do?" Moonsy asked, trying to maintain herself. She'd just lost one of her oldest friends, now her lover had tumbled down a stairway into a tunnel with Queen Corydalis's legendary hero and the sword she was sworn to protect.

"First we find a way up." Gallarael gave her a smile. "Then we find a different way down." She paused. "You should ride Poops, like Thorn used to." Gallarael turned and started shifting.

"It's the only way you'll be able to keep up with me," she added before leaning forward and bounding away on all fours.

Chapter Twenty-One

> In that land across the sea,
> a fierce dragon queen, she rose.
> But in the end the great High King,
> Removed her from his throne.
> – The Ballad of Ornspike

Vanx decided the borehole could have continued down, and the floor been built later, and he knew the old wizard that had sent him here in the first place was powerful enough to do such a thing. By the hells, Vanx could probably do it himself, without magic, if he had the laborers.

Vanx laughed at himself, for he knew detection spells, all sorts of spells really, it was just never his first instinct to use them. He cast a detection on the floor and found that it wasn't magicked, and then he realized that, even had it been built by arcane means, the magic might not have left a trace? What he did feel, the thing that was certainly full of magic, wasn't far down the man sized arch Chelda had just ducked into.

"Wait." Vanx cast a light spell. It sputtered and crackled and gave off an uneven, wavering illumination.

"Bah." Chelda barked out a laugh. "That is the best you can do? It flickers like a candle in the wind."

"Bah, yourself," Vanx grinned. It was a pathetic light spell, he knew, but unlike the one's the elves cast, it didn't announce their presence like a beacon. "What we are after is just at the end of this passage so watch for triggers."

"What is that?" Chelda asked as she came upon something.

The sound of her voice wasn't hopeful so Vanx squeezed past her to see for himself. *What is that?*

Sitting atop a crude stone pedestal was— was— was not what he expected. It was a dust covered, intricately carved wooden box.

"What the farkin' hells is in it?" Chelda asked.

"I've no idea." Vanx couldn't believe this was what was down here. A box covered in runes that he didn't understand? It was large enough to hold three gem seeds, but barely. He couldn't see a seam, or a way to open it.

Cautiously, he picked it up.

After a moment, Vanx sucked in a breath. He started shaking and fell toward Chelda, who caught him with terror in her eyes.

Vanx burst out laughing, and she dropped him. She nearly booted him in the chest on his way to the floor. Through his mirth he said, "Well it didn't just fill me with knowledge or anything, but it has markings."

"What do they say?" She glared dawn at him but, underneath, he could tell that all of her ill-tempered tension was dissipating.

"I have no idea." Vanx shrugged. Before he put the book sized item in his pouch he felt something rattling inside. Something heavy and with little room to wiggle. He could only hope it was one or more of the gem-seeds.

"Rukk will be able to read the box if Moonsy doesn't recognize the script? I'm worried though, the Goddess doesn't, has never, sent me on a fool's errand. Or maybe they are all fool's errands, I don't know, but she said that I would learn what I needed to learn here. Even if the box is a case, and the gem-seeds are in it, I still don't know where to take them."

"What do we do now? This is the end of this cavern, and I'm tired of stooping."

"Of course." Vanx indicated that she could lead the way out if she liked. He cast the detection again, just to be sure, and it was the same result. The thing here radiating all the magic was the thing now in his belt pack. He'd hoped to find a map, or a sentient being that would explain what he needed to know.

He sent out another feeling for Poops, which didn't raise a response from his dog. It was terrible not being able to feel his familiar. The idea that something might have happened to the pup began to creep into his thoughts.

As they exited the tunnel, into the bottom of the borehole, Chelda screamed. Vanx knew by the texture of her terror that there were spiders, and he cast a spell as he emerged.

It was more than one spider. There were a half-dozen of them, and they all had glowing crimson markings and angry red venom sacks ready to pump something full of deadly web silk with a sharp, dagger-long, spinneret.

At least they weren't as big as the first one he'd killed. Nevertheless, they were closing in, and all Chelda had to fight with was a close range basher. Vanx moved to put her between him and the annex they'd just emerged from. And then he unleashed his spell.

The closer of the things were decimated, but Vanx was suddenly exhausted. He had to fight to keep his wits while drawing his sword.

Two of the remaining spiders leapt on him. He saw the other had Chelda blocked. Chelda was fighting more than just the spider, he knew, and he was about to be stung because he didn't have the physical strength left to save himself. Casting all the spells had left him sapped. He should have been practicing to build up his strength, but he'd failed himself.

"I love you, Chel," he said weakly. "Moonsy and Gallarael, too."

Then he turned away from her demise and watched a spinneret ease down at his abdomen, taking aim. When it raised in a flash and came down to impale him, he clenched his eyes shut, and said a sharp prayer to the Goddess.

Chapter Twenty-Two

> Across his sea we sail,
> to Nepton we hold true.
> For if you cross old Nepton,
> his sea will swallow you.
> – A sailor's song

Vanx expected to feel the stinger but, instead, he felt Poops licking his face. He opened his eyes to see that they were at the foot of the circular stair well, a few dozen feet above the open hole leading down to where the spiders were.

"What the—?" he blurted.

"Shhh," Gallarael shushed. Her smile was a relief, but he thought he might be dead.

"I teleported you two out of harm's way," Moonsy said. "I sensed it, when you found the artifact. Once you did, the ramp reverted to stairs again."

Vanx hugged his dog and gave him a good belly rub when Poops laid down right beside him.

"He found a wooden box," Chelda dropped to a knee and hugged Moonsy.

After Poops's need for affection was sated, Gallarael helped Vanx to his feet. "So you found them?" She asked. "Where are the gem-seeds?"

"I found something, but it tells me nothing." Vanx was still trying to wrap his mind around the idea that a venomous spinneret had been a heartbeat away from ending him. "I think they may be inside the box. It is just the right size to hold three gems and it is heavy, but I can't read the markings or open it."

"We found something, too." She shrugged and grinned at Chelda. "While most of the rooms on the top floor were sleeping quarters, storage rooms, and a kitchen, one room was a study, and on the desk was this.

She unshouldered a pack and carefully pulled out an ancient book that had a spine as thick as his hand was wide. Its cover was tooled leather and the binding looked to be masterfully crafted. "I marked the page it was on with a bit of Moonsy's hair."

"Hey," the elven general snapped, patting at her head as if she would miss a single strand.

"It was opened on a picture of your jacaranda tree," she said as if she'd just solved the whole riddle. "It's a book about trees, but I can't read the language it's written in. Neither can she."

Vanx recognized the script immediately, but that was a disappointment. It was the same undecipherable language that was used to mark the box. The fact that Moonsy couldn't read the language solidified what they needed to do.

"The language is the key," said Vanx after flipping through a few pages. The book had carefully sketched renditions of different types of trees, some Vanx had seen, some he hadn't. Following each drawing, there were paragraphs of information and, in some instances, crude maps. "We need Master Ruuk, or an older Zythian linguist."

"See there," Moonsy said to Chelda and Gallarael, "you were both right."

"You were," Vanx agreed. "Something above and something below. And now we need to set sail, for I believe the book will tell us how to open the box, and everything else we need to know. Once we can read it, that is."

Vanx was hopeful now. With the seeds and a book full of directions, they could finish what they started.

"I thought you weren't leaving this island until you explored it all," Chelda said. "There is a whole section we've yet to even set eyes on."

"But we have what we need, Chel," Vanx shrugged. "Why bother?"

"Yah," she agreed but still sounded disappointed.

"Ruuk might tell us we have to go fight goblins wherever we smash the next seed, or something," he offered.

"You think so?" her tone brightened, and Moonsy laughed at them both. Vanx couldn't tell if Moonsy was just hiding her emotion, or if she'd really put Anitha's death behind her. It was hard to read an elf, but looking at her gave him an idea.

"Maybe so, Chel." He couldn't help but grin. "General Moonseed, can you ride one of the great hawks to Zyth from here?"

"Take the book to Master Ruuk, you mean?"

"Yup." Vanx nodded.

"I don't see why not." She shrugged. "I'd want the other hawk to go along."

"Of course." Vanx started to suggest that one of the others could go, too, but Chelda was just too big, and Gallarael, well, he figured she'd be better suited to helping here if they stayed and waited on Moonsy.

They started up the stairs, Chelda and Moonsy in the lead, with Vanx and Poops beside them. Gallarael was behind him so he turned and asked her the question that had just popped into his head.

"You guys didn't happen to check the floors between here and the top did you?"

"There were five of them, counting the level we came in on," Gallarael said. "We looked around the second floor and saw nothing but a ceremonial altar and a few more sleeping areas. Then Moonsy rode Poops up the ramp. The other levels had no torches so we left them alone."

"Moonsy rode Poops?" Vanx was amazed. "Like Thorn?"

"Yes, and Poops loved it."

"We'll not be waiting to smash goblins, Vanxy," Chelda yelled from about a half turn ahead of them. There was a loud cracking *thump* and a mannish looking thing, made from some sort of magicked stone, fell past them, crashing and breaking on the stairs as it continued down. "Hurry, I can only hold them a moment more."

It was all Vanx could do to get himself up and onto the landing. He saw there were a handful of gargoyles, not goblins, blocking their way. They'd come from one of the darkened levels above them. Chelda had them crouching back, afraid to get walloped by her war hammer. Vanx saw at least three crumbled stone legs when he slid behind her. He also saw Moonsy, just inside the archway, ready to blast anything that followed her lover in after them.

Chapter Twenty-Three

> Deep in a stormy meadow,
> as the lightning crashes down.
> I fight through all my sorrow,
> for deep in mourning I'll be found.
> – A Zythian bard's song

Chelda was visibly disappointed when Moonsy blasted the three, stone formed gargoyles into rubble and lit the whole floor up with her bright illumination spell.

Everyone else was just happy no more of the things remained. The room they were in, for that is all it was, had a bunk with a skeleton in it. The man was still wearing his night clothes, though he'd have to had been there a hundred years or more to be so decayed.

Vanx saw a handwritten note on the bedside table. There was a quill and an ink bottle there, too. Vanx picked up the inkwell first, and wasn't surprised to find its contents were long evaporated.

"He must have written it on his deathbed," Gallarael said, stealing the thought from Vanx's mind.

The clay ink jar shattered on the floor and Vanx swore. Something must have been living in it. He was certain something had crawled out and bit him, but he saw nothing of the sort.

He grabbed the piece of parchment and grunted when he saw it was also written in a language he had never seen before. He unshouldered the bag he'd taken from Gallarael, opened the ancient tome, and replaced Moonsy's hair with the dead man's note. It was time get out of there.

"Can you just blast our way up out of here Moonsy?" Vanx asked. "Chelda can follow and smash anything left moving. Then, as soon we get outside, keep your light right over us until we get to Gallarael's tunnel. I will take care of that wyrm if it comes."

"You'll end up a wyrm turd yet." Chelda grinned. She liked the plan.

A few more gargoyles tried to block their passage, but Moonsy dispatched them with ease. It was a strange tentacle-like vine, reaching from inside the middle level's archway that caused all the chaos.

Vanx cast a powerful blasting spell at the thing as it wrapped around Moonsy. It seemed aware she was the cause of the light, but Vanx didn't know how he knew that. When his spell impacted the sparsely leafed trailer, it only made it get bigger.

He jumped over another grasping tendril, but it missed him. He saw Poops get wrapped around by it, though.

"Pound it, Chel," he yelled. "Find its base and pound the shit out of it!"

Vanx used his sword to cut Poops free, but Moonsy was another matter. She must have been losing consciousness for the strength of her light spell was fading.

Gallarael, her skin now hard and glossy black, flashed dagger long claws as she followed Chelda into the arch. Vanx wasn't repulsed enough to let it distract him from his intention, this time. He did a cartwheel, being careful to keep his blade under control, and then pushed off the banister in an attempt to get a clean cut, but the banister gave way.

Vanx's sword cut something, but as he crashed into the stairs, he could only hope it wasn't Moonsy. He looked to see, but the light from her spell was gone.

Vanx cast a light into being then, a fairly bright one for his ability. He heard Chelda's pounding and Gallarael's growling snarl coming from the darkness and wondered how Chelda could see. Gallarael, he knew, could see like a creature, just as he could when he submerged into Poops senses, and Poops was emitting deep concern over Moonsy.

Vanx saw her, and was glad that he hadn't cut her in half as he'd feared. He must have cut the tendril for there were a few purple splotched green leaves and some sappy looking goo near the elf.

Vanx thought she might be dead, but he held out hope and poked her with the Glaive of Gladiolus.

"Yah," he heard Chelda shout in victory.

He had never been happier to see anything when Moonsy's eyelids fluttered open.

The elf reached out and grabbed one of the leaves. She seemed transfixed by the strange pattern. Vanx looked at a leaf more closely. It was like any other light green, heart shaped viny leaf, only these looked to have been splattered with lavender and plum dye.

"Pretty," she mumbled. Then she got to her feet, recast her light spell, and called for her lover.

"Are you all right, Chel?" she asked.

"Yah, I am," Chelda responded. "Come look at this."

Vanx could tell that whatever it was had Chelda amazed. It had to be extra spectacular for Gallarael to stay silent about it. Or maybe she was still in her partially formed hide?

Vanx decided it didn't matter and followed Moonsy through the archway to see what they'd discovered. He wasn't ready for what hit him. Only the fact that Poops darted in a few seconds before he did, kept him from being overwhelmed by it all.

Chapter Twenty-Four

Cold words cut like a knife,
sharp and hard, they'll steal a life.
They'll tear a heart open wide,
and leave nothing left but pain inside.
– Broken, a Zythian ballad

A massive forest spread out before them. Over the potent smell of pollen and vegetation, the smell of brine and jacaranda bells filled his and Poops's nostrils. In the far distance, Vanx could see the the ocean and, by the lay of the land, he figured they were back in the section of the island where they'd come ashore.

He was amazed. It had to have been some sort of portal. He saw the remains of the plant that had reached in and gotten hold of Poops and Moonsy, and he shook his head. The idea that something rooted out here could reach inside the arch was hard to conceive, but it had just happened.

And where was here? he wondered. The dragon's lazing stone wasn't behind them. They hadn't just stepped out of the strange building. They were standing in an ancient looking archway, built atop an elevated clearing.

Vanx had to give it to whoever created such a passage, they picked an amazing vantage point, with a breathtaking view, to do it.

"What is that?" he wondered aloud. He could see tiny streamers in the sky with something attached at the bottom. They were drifting in the air. The wind carried some toward them, but they were moving lazily, as if they might never come down.

"Look over there," Chelda said. "What are they doing? What are they?"

Vanx watched as one of the streamers, then another, landed in the branches of a tree across the valley. Slowly, the leaves of a branch were clouded, and then browned.

Then Vanx saw one of them drifting down at them. He was stricken with fear when he saw what they were. It was one of the baby red spiders. They were all drifting on the wind on stringers of web as long as his arm.

A few more moments of panicked looking confirmed his assessment of where they were, for the jacaranda tree could be made out, its top poking over one of three ridges that lay between them and the sea. The spiders sparked away in hot sizzling pops when they drifted too close to it, but Vanx sensed pain coming from the tree, pain from where the sea breeze came over the ridge, stripping its leaves and burning its bark.

What had he done? The jacaranda tree might not have supposed to been released here. Now, more than ever, he needed to know what the book said.

"Do not let them land on us!" Vanx warned. "Those are the ones that almost killed Zeezle. I must have launched them out of that tube when I blasted their mother."

The phenomenon happened a little closer to them this time. A spider's streamer caught in a branch, and the spider quickly started constructing a web. The silk cocoons weren't that big, just enough to cover a dozen leaves or so, but those leaves quickly turned brown, and this was happening in thousands of places across the forest. It was as if cottony balls were blooming, then browning, all around them.

The place on his hand where he thought he'd been bitten itched, but still he saw no mark or even any redness other than that caused by his scratching.

As he gathered himself and pondered the situation, Vanx heard Chelda gasp in concern, and he turned.

She was looking at him with terror in her eyes.

Vanx felt Poops, then. The dog was hurting on his right forepaw, just about where Vanx had been scratching.

Poops wobbled and fell over. Vanx drew the glaive and stabbed the dog. This seemed to help, but only for a time. Vanx understood, this. The poison was still in Poops, so even after the glaive healed him, the poison would start taking effect all over again. The dog needed a real healing spell.

"The hawks, are not responding, Vanx." Moonsy's sadness seemed to have returned tenfold. He doubted she knew Poops was hurt.

"Cast a protection to keep the drifting spiders off us, and keep Poops alive with the glaive while you work a proper healing. I'll try to call the hawks." Vanx grabbed the Hoar Witch's crystal dangling at his neck and reached out to the remaining two great hawks.

Something responded to his call, but it was that strange coral colored wyrm, he was sure of it.

"They aren't there, or—" He sighed. "We need to go straight to the coast, I can call the *Adventurer* to meet us." He pointed in a direction opposite the newly formed Heart Tree.

Maybe a half-day's hike away was what looked like a sandy beach.

"Poops is not well," the elf said, but he has no bite. "I'm not sure what to do."

"Heal him," Vanx said a little more sharply than he intended.

Moonsy did her best, then she spent a long time casting protective and defensive wards on the whole group.

"Rest yourselves—" Vanx was interrupted as one of the drifting spiders came in contact with Monsy's protective spell and sizzled away.

Vanx decided that he could wait to get back on the ship to sleep, and poor Poops wasn't getting worse, but the dog wasn't feeling any better either. "Never mind. Moonsy, you keep the glaive out for Poops. I'll carry him. No doubt we will have to return to right the wrong I must have done here." Vanx grunted as he heaved Poops up to his chest. It was disheartening to see all the webs in the trees now. They were everywhere.

"We need to find out what this book says before we do anything else." Vanx started down. "We need to understand it all."

Chapter Twenty-Five

> Anytime I'm fishing,
> and my line is in the water.
> Nothing really matters,
> but the bobble of my bobber.
> – A fisherman's song

As they made their way through the forest, Vanx wondered about the bite. He was sure he'd seen something bite him, but the effect happened to his familiar. Or maybe Poops had been bitten, and Vanx felt the bite. What he saw might have been a flake of dried ink from the inkpot.

He knew he had to start practicing the spells he'd learned from the Hoar Witch's books. After his Goddess implied it wasn't the nature of a spell, but the intention of its using that mattered, he was less reserved about casting them. Right now, though, he was mostly concerned with keeping his dog alive. Poops was getting better, and the swelling going down, but he still wasn't healed. Vanx could feel his four-legged friend's unease, but at the moment, Poops wanted off the island as much as he'd ever wanted anything.

Vanx and Chelda took turns carrying the dog, and they made the beach just as the sun left half a moon in the sky to light their way.

By the time they reached the beach, Ronzon, and more likely, the magical *Adventurer,* herself, had made their way around the shoreline to greet them.

For a few moments, they all stood there on the beach, looking at each other.

"There is no rowboat," Chelda observed.

"It's called a longboat, or a dinghy," Vanx corrected.

"Do you think I care what it is called?" Chelda barked.

"I bet you a gold piece you'll say longboat or dinghy next time," he joked through an icy cold sweat, and he knew she would.

"Moonsy, can you get us over there?" Vanx handed Poops off to Chelda, and patted the shoulder satchel he'd been using to carry the old book with. "We wouldn't want this to get wet," he reminded.

The next thing he knew he was landing on the deck of his ship, his dog familiar and Chelda right beside him as his knees hit the deck wood, hard.

Gallarael followed, then Moonsy appeared.

The *Adventurer* didn't wait for a command, sails unfurled, and rigging snapped tight of its own accord. It knew they were headed for the Isle of Zyth.

Vanx carried Poops down to their quarters and sat him in the bed. The dog licked him in thanks, but looked miserable. Vanx asked Ronzon to make some broth from the bouillon they'd stocked, and a lot of it. Ronzon was happy to, for Chelda was in the galley eating everything she could, and Ronzon knew she'd tell him what happened on the island.

Vanx used the glaive as he had on Zeezle, stabbing Poops every few minutes until the swelling went away. It was odd to Vanx that pus and webby stuff hadn't oozed out of a bite hole the way Zeezle's wound had healed. It was then that Vanx decided that neither he nor the dog had been bitten by one of the red spiders, but maybe something else. He also decided he was feeling the same sickly feeling his familiar was, only he had mistaken it for spell weariness, or maybe it was a combination of spell weariness and some sort of venom or poison. Whatever it was, the glaive and Moonsy's spells didn't fully heal it.

Vanx felt better by morning, but he and Poops were holding close to each other through their familiar link because they both knew something wasn't right.

*

The next afternoon, a storm rolled in, so everyone was below, in the galley. It barely fit them all. In fact, it didn't. Chelda was sitting on the stairs that led up to the main deck, looking in as she told an emphatic tale.

Vanx had opened a pony keg of good rum and listened as Chelda told Ronzon, again, all they had been through.

As he guessed, Chelda didn't sugarcoat the events or how they unfolded, but to Vanx's surprise, Moonsy didn't wince, or even show emotion, when the parts about Anitha being munched by the dragon and the strange disappearance of the great hawks were told.

Vanx had a nagging feeling in the back of his skull. He hoped they could get back in time to save all those trees from the spider webbings. After all, it was he who had blasted all the little spiders out of a borehole, like a buffoon. He made to scratch at his hand and found he's scraped it deep enough that there was now a scab.

He looked at it curiously and thought about the clay inkwell falling to the floor. The way it shattered. The dullness of the thud. And then he heard Chelda's sudden silence. He looked at the others and they had followed her eyes to rest on him.

She must have asked me a question, Vanx thought, right before he fell face first into the end of the table.

Vanx opened his eyes to the hovering concern on the faces of three beautiful women. His dog was already beside him. He felt fine, but he knew he'd been sweating.

"I poked you with the glaive Vanx, and it hasn't helped much," Moonsy said. "Too bad we don't have a few Medika's here to ease your symptoms. As uncomfortable as you and Poops look, according to the glaive, you are well."

Chelda, who stooped and used the wall the stay balanced as the ship pitched and rolled with the sea, gave Vanx a look of concern he'd rarely ever seen on her. In fact, the last time he'd seen her expression so serious was when she was in her home village, around her father.

"I saw a spider on you Vanx," she said. "A little tiny one, with some blue stripes on its back."

"When?" Vanx asked.

Gallarael leaned down and gave him a kiss, and then she rolled her eyes Chelda's way. The look indicated the gargan might be a little confused. "She says she saw it when we stepped out of that dragonstone, and again the other day, right before you banged your head on the table."

"The other day?" Vanx sat up and immediately regretted it. He felt Poops urging him to lay down. Their familiar link was growing stronger and stronger. "How long have I—?"

"Two full nights, and this is the third evening." She smiled when he resettled himself. He missed her golden hair and, for a moment or two, he wondered what might have happened had her lover Trevin survived the ogre war in Dyntalla. Would she still be in love with him?

"We'll be at Little Haven on the morrow." Moonsy harrumphed to remind Vanx and Gallarael that she and Chelda were still in the room. "The glaive is there." She pointed to his belt. It was hanging on the desk chair's nearest stile, easily within reach. "Use it if you think it will help, but it has done nothing but heal the worry wound you've worn into your hand."

"Vanx, I saw a little blue spider on you," Chelda was more adamant this time.

"I believe you Chel," Vanx said. "I'll strip down and have a hot soak and even scrub my skivvy's" He gave her the best smile he could. "I'll have to look my best for Molly."

"Who, by my brother's falcon, is Molly?" Gallarael snapped.

Chelda laughed away her severity. "It is from one of the songs Vanx sings, Gal. Take a deep breath. Come Moonsy, let's let Vanx get cleaned up."

"Thanks, Chelda." Vanx was serious. "I'll double check my gear after I bathe."

"Yah." Chelda seemed relieved now. "Don't just wash the skivvy's, Vanxy. Wash the rest of your clothes as well."

"Hmm." he gave Gallarael a look. "Do I stink?"

"You scared us when you went down." She nodded her head. "We all thought it was a bite, like Chelda said, because you were pale and sweaty for a good while. You mumbled stuff." With this she grinned. "You mumbled my name a few times." She kissed his forehead and reached over him to give Poops's head a rub.

"I'll get some water heating and have Ronzon bring down the tub."

"Don't bother heating the water," he said. "I need to practice using spells."

"Yes," she nodded again. "Yes, according to Chelda, you do."

Chapter Twenty-Six

> Deep under the deep,
> and deeper in the ground.
> That is where you'll find yourself,
> if you wander around a fairy mound.
> – A rim rider campfire song

After managing to heat the water to a boil, Vanx went through his clothes while he waited for it to cool. At one point, out of the corner of his eye, he thought he might have seen a little blue bug, dart into the folds of something, but he wasn't sure, and eventually decided he was seeing things.

He even went through the shoulder bag containing the old book and the wooden box. But he found no spiders.

He took some time to wash his long hair. Then he soaked for a while. When he was finished washing the rest of himself, with lye soap and a handled scrubber, the water was a murky brown.

Vanx practiced another spell and vanquished the filthy water from the tub out into the sea. He then found a clean sark, put it on, and carried the water bucket up into the starlit night. He wanted to fetch some fresh water from the barrel to wash his clothes in.

"You're alive then," Ronzon said, startling Vanx. He was so sure that the *Adventurer* was taking care of the sailing that he'd almost forgotten Ronzon was up here.

"I am." Vanx grinned. "But barely. Never go adventuring with three women. It isn't worth it."

"I heard that," came an elven sounding voice. Vanx looked up to see Moonsy in the crow's nest, looking out across the dark choppy water with one of the tubes.

"If you shutter the lantern, you'll see better," Vanx told her, and she did so.

"When will we see the cliffs?" Vanx asked Ronzon. Sailing into Little Haven was sometimes tricky, for it was just a narrow passage between cliffs.

"This ship owns the sea, Vanx." Ronzon spoke as if he were proud to be the *Adventurer's* deckhand. "We'll not even need to touch that wheel, I bet'cha."

"We'll see." Vanx nodded. "Have you ever sailed into Little Haven? Have you ever been to Zyth?"

"Been to Flotsam a time or two," Ronzon shrugged. "Do they have the strider races in Little Haven? Them kanga beasts them heathens ride are amazing."

Ronzon didn't seem to remember that Vanx was half-Zythian, but the racial comment didn't bother Vanx anymore. It must have, Moonsy though. She cast a spell, that sent down a little strand of magic that captured the seaman's attention. He and Vanx stood at the rail, watching raptly as the sparkling string, twisted and turned. Then it folded into a thin knot, moved closer to Ronzon, and snapped the mesmerized sailor right in the nose.

"He is half-heathen, man." Moonsy's severity was feigned. "And Zeezle is a full blooded man-eater. You'd better watch yourself."

Ronzon was wide eyed, and Vanx thought he might have been afraid enough to cry, but when he saw the jest in Vanx's face, and heard the mirth in Moonsy's laugh, he accepted that he deserved what he'd gotten.

"Sorry," Ronzon dropped his head. "It's just sailor talk."

"It's all right." Vanx patted the man on the shoulder. "But don't let Zeezle hear it. He might try and make a stew of you. There is a racing pit outside of town, maybe after we find a translator, we will have time to go to the track. It will take a while to go through the whole book."

With that, Vanx went back down, returned twice more to get more water, and then latched his cabin door behind him. He hadn't noticed Gallarael, laying on his bunk, all naked and lithe, smiling up at him.

"I like it when you're clean," she grinned, rolled over, and used her biceps to squeeze and accentuate her ample cleavage in an inviting way.

Vanx couldn't resist her, and Poops leapt from the bunk to allow them room. The dog lapped clean water from the bucket, then turned a circle on the floor before getting comfortable.

"Come, Vanx." Gallarael growled. He went to her, pulling off his sark as he went. He slid into bunk beside her and relished the feel of her hot skin against his.

The idea of her changeling skin, slipped into his mind, but he fought the revulsion. In fact, he relied on that sickening emotion to keep him from climaxing, over and over again, every time he was about to come, he thought about her slick, hardened, glossy black hide.

The method proved to be effective, for they made love long into the night and, when Vanx finally filled her with his seed, it felt as if the end of his manhood had exploded in a bone tingling burst of ecstatic elation.

He must have fallen asleep, for he woke naked in his bunk, with his arm around Poops, to Ronzon's excited call of, "Land Ho!" coming from above.

He didn't feel good, and neither did Poops, but he stabbed the dog, and then himself with the glaive, and got dressed. It made them feel better, but there was something wrong, and Vanx hoped he could find a linguist and a healer, thus solving all their problems at once.

The nagging feeling that the jacaranda Heart Tree was in pain, and the forest around it, needed him, was in the back of his skull, too.

He knew they didn't have time to dally.

Chapter Twenty-Seven

> Old Master Wiggins,
>   finally died of gout,
>   but he wouldn't fit a coffin,
>   'cause his leg was sticking out.
>
> – A Parydon street ditty

Amakra Malic passed away when Vanx was thirty-six years old. She was taken by a merciless wasting disease that was exclusive to those of Zythian blood. It was a sudden thing. One year, she was glowing and full of life, the next she was a withered husk, empty of all but love for her only son. She was young by Zythian standards, barely a hundred years old. Her life had caused a hurricane of emotion to assail the hearts and minds of the Zythian elders, and not just because of her choice of an infamous human mate. In her life, Vanx's mother had challenged ancient customs and pushed the boundaries of the old ways at every opportunity.

They warned that her mixed-blood child would be stillborn, just as scores of others had been in the past. They said her heart would break when she outlived her lover and was forced to watch him die. They said the Goddess would shun her for breaking so many traditions, and that she could only be considered Zythian because of her blood.

Vanx's birth changed all of that. He wasn't stillborn, and his father died at sea on a merchant ship taken by pirates off the coast of Harthgar. Her husband never had the chance to grow old before her eyes.

The Goddess smiled upon her brightly enough that she lived to see her son mature. Some said her death was a punishment for the life she lived, but she told Vanx from her deathbed, that her life had been a great and wondrous happening. She'd known love; she'd turned heads and raised eyebrows.

She knew she had given birth to an impossible child who was touched by the Goddess herself. And she always said her life had been full of joy and triumph.

"Remember who and what you are, Vanx," she'd whispered.

By then, only her smile and the light shining in her eyes marked her as his mother. The rest of her was shriveled and discolored. "The humans will envy you for being part Zythian, and the Zythians for being part human. You must rise above them, for what other people think of you matters very little. It's what you think of yourself that matters."

Those words echoed in Vanx's ears now as he let his eyes focus back on the sea. He took a few moments to blink away the tears brought on by his mother's memory, and then took the wheel of the *Adventurer*, just in case she needed a little help.

There were several types of birds clinging to the watermarked cliff faces that rose up like fortress walls out of the sea. There were smaller birds that would dart out in bunches and larger birds that would swoop through the smaller flocks trying to eat them.

There were also small sea dactyls that dove deep into schools of bait only to surface with gullets full of floundering prey.

Vanx was pleased with the way the *Adventurer* handled the narrow passage, and even the docks. Vanx could feel it drawing from his mind, and wondered if his father had been connected to his ship, *Foamfollower*, in such a way.

Vanx also felt that he and Poops were in need of a Zythian healer so, as they neared the dock, he had Moonsy teleport herself all the way to the top of the switchback to fetch one. There was no way Vanx or his puny feeling pup could manage the climb.

"Sir Earlin made that climb in full plate armor," Vanx told Chelda.

The two of them sat with their legs dangling off the side of the ship, near the bow. They were using the rail for an arm rest, Chelda, the top rail, and Vanx the mid rail. Her size was drawing some attention, but it was him the Zythians all wanted to set eyes on.

"Yah." Chelda nodded approvingly. They yellow eyes of the dockhands bothered Chelda, Vanx could tell. But for whatever reason, Zeezle's eyes, or Master Ruuk's, which were just as yellow and feral as those around them, hadn't ever seemed to make her uneasy.

"He wasn't even winded at the top." Vanx shook his head in disbelief, but it was the truth. "Do you think Ronzon will return?"

"He'll be back," Chelda snorted. "He watches me and Moonsy through the keyhole. Besides, Gallarael went up there with him."

"Want me to get rid of him?" Vanx was nauseous, and Poops couldn't seem to drink enough water. Vanx still had to clean the turf box and pay the rude Zythians swapping out their empty water barrels for full ones.

"Nah." She smiled at him. "His skills would be hard to replace, and he's familiar with the ship."

One of the loaders working another boat called Vanx, "The Sea Witch's get," and spat at the dock near them.

Chelda started to go after him but Vanx stopped her.

"I am the Sea Witch's get," he said to her alone. "My mother sailed with my father for years. Being that she was Zythian, she was strange to the seamen. She was known as the Sea Witch, and only because I was due to be born did she not sail with my father on his final, fatal voyage."

"That's deep," Chelda said.

Her poor attempt at wordplay, and the goofy smile on her face made Vanx laugh despite the way he was feeling. She'd heard this all before, and more than once.

He felt the urge to vomit, and he could feel the beads of icy sweat dripping down his brow. He was hoping Moonsy could find a good healer, but he was never happier to see Master Ruuk appear on the planking, scaring the rude seamen into curses.

Chapter Twenty-Eight

> I cast this wreath into the sea,
> to satisfy Nepton.
> Shelter well into your depths,
> the souls you've taken on.
> – a prayer to the god of the sea

"Moonsy should be along soon, with a friend of mine," Master Ruuk explained as he came aboard. "We are picking up goods here for the rebuilding. I would call it pure luck that we happened to be here on the same day as you, but with you, Vanx, I think there is no such thing as coincidence."

"I don't know what any of that means, Master." Vanx had to use the rail as he led the older Zythian magi below deck. "I'm here because I need help deciphering a language I've never seen before."

"You look like you need more than that my friend," said Master Ruuk. "The Zythian I sent Moonsy to fetch, is older than the both of use combined, and quite knowledgeable.

"May I have a look?" he asked once they were inside Vanx's cabin.

They sat opposite each other in the booth. Master Ruuk opened the book to the page marked by the note Vanx had placed there, but he sat the book down and grabbed Vanx's hands instead of reading.

Vanx felt a tingling rush of energy sweep through his system, and he felt Poops, enjoying the same. Ruuk must have cast a healing of some sort on them.

"I'm not sure what has gotten you, Vanx," the old Zythian said. "I sense there is something in your blood, but to call it poison would be inaccurate. I'll ponder it while I look at this."

Master Ruuk put the note aside and marveled at the jacaranda tree sketch. "You know these trees hate the salty air blowing directly on them, yet they grow near the sea?"

Vanx hadn't known that, and now he understood the trees agony. He should have cracked that seed deeper in the valley, closer to the lake. He wondered if he'd made a terrible mistake and whether the tree killing spiders he launched across the island had killed the entire forest by now.

"Yes, yes, this language is, well I'm not even sure it is a language. But this," he grabbed the parchment they'd found by the skeleton inside the dragon's lazing stone, "this I can read."

"What does it say?" Vanx was already feeling ill again, but a rush of excitement had come over him. He saw Chelda sitting on the stairs, listening in, and knew she was as curious as he was.

"It says, 'Beware, once bitten, humanity is lost. You'll become a slave to the Goss, as I have. If you're reading this, it is too late for you anyway. Kalzafranta Murr.'"

Poops indicated he'd heard something coming from the satchel. Vanx immediately went for the strange box, they found. The thing that radiated all the power. To his surprise, it was open.

Carefully, not to drop the gem seeds, he held the box so they wouldn't spill, and sat it on the table. To his grave disappointment, when he opened the lid, there were no gem seeds inside, only a gold looking-glass that was missing its lens. It had the same unfamiliar markings as the book carved around the handle.

Vanx met Master Ruuk's gaze and found the old man's curiosity was now stoked. Then they heard a click, coming from the box. Vanx couldn't help but try and figure out what had caused it.

Vanx couldn't find what made the sound, but he suddenly felt better, and so did Poops. An idea struck him then, and he closed the lid of the box, with the golden artifact inside.

As he guessed the box locked closed.

"Read those last words again, Master Ruuk," Vanx asked.

"Kalzafranta Murr," Master Ruuk said, and the box popped open. Vanx thought about it for a moment and decided that wasn't the sound he'd heard but, nevertheless, he closed the lid and spoke the words himself. He was pleased to see that the box opened, and he found a parchment and quill, and wrote the words down so he wouldn't forget them.

"What is a Goss?" Vanx asked. He did feel better. It was as if he'd never been ill, Poops had already squeezed past Chelda to go lap more water and shit in his turf box.

"A type of spider I think," Master Ruuk answered, unaware that his response had chilled Vanx to the core.

"A very dangerous spider," came an elderly voice from the deck above. "No, dear," the old man said as he stepped around Chelda's huge form. "I think I can, there, yes." A silver haired, bright, yellow-eyed old Zythian was suddenly in the room.

Moonsy negotiated Chelda with a lot more grace and entered behind him. And everyone paused, waiting for him to respond.

Chapter twenty-Nine

> When it comes to dragons,
> you can never know.
> One might let you ride its back,
> while the next might eat you whole.
> -- A dragon's song

"The Goss is a legendary thing, and if there is a looking glass in that case, then I'd guess you've long been bitten."

"I told you there was a spider, Vanx." Chelda started. "But how could *you* know that," she asked the newcomer?

Vanx looked around the others and held up his hand, indicating for Chelda to hold her tongue for the time being. Begrudgingly, she acknowledged him.

"This is Master Beriinga," Master Ruuk offered. "Master Beriinga, this is Vanx of Malic, General Gloryvine Moonseed, and Chelda Flar."

"To answer your question, Chelda Flar, I've read a lot of books, dear." He eased into the bench seat beside Master Ruuk. Vanx let Moonsy slide in beside him. "I've never seen this one, but I have heard about it. It is called the Tome of Arbor, and within its pages are the secrets of the trees." He carefully turned the book so that it was at the end of the table and all of them, save for Chelda, could see the tome in proper orientation.

He began thumbing through the pages until he found an image of a poplar tree with web worms growing in its limbs. "Is this what you were seeing?" he asked Moonsy, who must have explained their dilemma on the way here.

"It is," Vanx and the elf answered in unison.

"And they were red marked arachnoids, you saw?" He paused and frowned. "This isn't good." The elderly Zythian stopped as if he was pondering something. He then mumbled something Vanx picked up through Poops keen hearing. "Usually caterpillars do this sort of thing, not arachnoids."

In the silence, Master Ruuk said, "This explains the sickness you've had. If you've been bitten I mean."

"As to that," since you are not a human, you will not meet the same dismal end as the man who wrote this." Master Beriinga indicated the note. "Your mixed blood should defy the full power of the Goss."

"But I'm not feeling ill now," Vanx proclaimed. "Poops feels well, too."

The two Zythians sat quiet for long moments. Master Beriinga finally indicated the box. "When did you first open it?" He was asking Vanx, but Master Ruuk answered.

"Just a few moments before you arrived," Ruuk told him.

"And after that is when you started feeling better?" he asked Vanx, who nodded.

"Then open the case, Vanx of Malic, and we may see if the legend of the Gossamer Lens is only a legend or if it is real."

Vanx wasn't sure about all the cryptic talk, and he didn't think it would matter, so he complied with the old Zythian.

"Kalzafranta Murr," Vanx said, and the lid to the box popped open. To his great surprise, there was a tiny blue spider spinning a web inside the ring of the looking glass.

"Oh my," Moonsy exclaimed. "There is your little blue spider, Chel."

Vanx watched in shocked awe as the little arachnoid finished spinning a web that spanned the ring, and then moved itself into a tiny spider symbol on the handle that Vanx hadn't made out before. There was an audible click, and the piece of metal the spider was on flipped around.

For the briefest moment, Vanx saw that, inside the handle, was where the spider lived. It must have left his person and gone to the handle while he and Ruuk were lost in wonder earlier.

"It lives in the handle?" Moonsy asked, though it was clear it was a rhetorical question.

Vanx picked up the looking glass and tried to read the text in the book. He was disappointed that it wasn't that easy.

Instead of the words appearing to make sense, the webs began to shimmer and swirl. Vanx was drawn into a vortex that reached into his mind as it beckoned him to look deeper into the web formed lens.

Vanx eventually saw the inked image of the spider web covered limbs shaking in the breeze. Just as he'd heard the jacaranda tree, he heard the trees with the web wrapped limbs screaming in pain. They were being suffocated by the silky constructions. The leaves unable to feel the sun, and gather rain, to generate the stuff a tree needed to survive.

Red wormy things wiggled in the webbing as they quickly grew into something else.

Vanx was transfixed. Especially when he saw what looked like Moonsy sitting on Chelda's shoulders, going from tree to tree with a torch, burning away the webs.

The sound of the jacaranda tree's pain could be heard in the distance of the vision, and he thumbed back to the image of the newest Heart Tree. In that image, he saw several robed men, chanting and circling the trunk, until the tree disappeared. It re-appeared some distance down slope, near the water's edge, and the men cheered in triumph.

The vision ended then, and the webbing in the lens was momentarily blue and glowing, but the thin stuff burned away, leaving the ring as empty as it was when Vanx first opened its case.

"Did you see?" Vanx asked.

"No, I saw nothing," answered Moonsy, who had the best chance of viewing what Vanx had seen.

The two Zythian's both shook their heads in the negative. "The seeing is only for the bitten," the older Zyth said.

"I need some spell casters, Master Ruuk." Vanx was suddenly sure of three things. "Enough to teleport a Heart Tree a few hundred feet without killing it, and who can use small controlled fire spells to burn away all the webs."

The first thing Vanx knew was, that to save the forest on the invisible island, they would have to go burn the spider webs out of the trees themselves, be it by magic, or by torch, as he'd seen in the vision, but that would be after they relocated the Heart Tree, for if that wasn't done in the next few days, it might be too late to save it.

That is where the third thing he now understood, came into play. The whole of the world was coming undone. He could feel it in his blood. The towers had bound it before but, before men possessing far too much power created those, the Heart Trees had held it all together. At the moment, there were only four Heart Trees living. The one at Saint Elm's Deep, the one in Harthgar, the one they'd quickened on Dragon Isle, and the newly formed jacaranda Heart Tree. And it was suffering terribly due to Vanx's haste and his lack of knowledge.

They didn't have that much time to finish quickening the remaining gem-seeds, so that their roots could find each other in the core. And now, Vanx and Poops were tied to the little blue spider, called the Goss, and it was making sure they sensed the full need for urgency. The webbed lens had only showed him what he needed to know. It didn't have to tell him that three more seeds still needed to be found, but he hoped the book, or the Goss, or the looking-glass, would know, and show him. But before they could even start, they had to fix Vanx's ignorant mistake.

If the jacaranda tree died, it was all for naught.

And with that thought, the full weight of Castovanti, Papri, and Anitha's lives weighed on Vanx's heart, for they were senseless deaths and Vanx felt responsible for all of them.

Chapter Thirty

> They've eyes like cats and skin that sheds,
> and golden hair upon their heads.
> They live forever I swear it's true,
> no telling what they'll do to you.
> – A sailor's song

The six Zythian spell casters Master Ruuk rounded up, took turns focusing the wind on the *Adventurer's* sails. They ranged in skill level from novice, to master, and just about all stages between. Though there were two that seemed as powerful as Master Rukk, or at least they seemed his age.

The elder Zythian, Master Beriinga, stayed behind, to make sure the refugees relying on he and Master Ruuk's rebuilding efforts didn't suffer, but he gladly helped round up this group. Vanx could only hope it would be enough.

The Zythians seemed well prepared to rid the trees of the webs. They'd brought down long, spear-like poles, rigged to hold a torch at the end, and A-frame ladders, but that wasn't all they were here for. Vanx laughed at the trickery Ruuk had resorted to. Of course the group knew they would be attempting to relocate a grown tree, as well as rid a forest of tree spiders, but the lake dragon that might try and eat them while they did so was never mentioned. Nor was the lazing stone, or the strange light-colored wyrm who lived there, but Vanx didn't remember if he'd even told Ruuk about that wondrous creature.

Vanx waited until long after dark, when, Ronzon and a younger Zyth were the only two on deck. Gallarael had brought two wreaths to the ship for him, and he had them now, one in each hand.

Poops followed him to the rail and watched curiously. The ship lifted slowly with the swell of the waves, and then slid down into the trough smoothly. Vanx spoke a prayer for his mother and dropped one of the woven floral rings into the dark cobalt sea. Next, he said a prayer for his father and tossed the other.

He stood there for a few long moments, thinking about the visions of his father the Hoar Witch had shown him. That was the only time he'd ever seen the man. He didn't know if he'd have the stones to willingly go down with his ship, as his father had, and wondered who would.

Oddly, he wasn't afraid of such a happening, just unsure how he would face it. Obviously, he was pledged to the Goddess's task, and more-or-less bound to it all now, by the bite of the Goss, so he couldn't just willingly die until all of that was done.

The little blue spider must have known someone would eventually read the note that contained the words to unlock the box, Vanx mused. He wondered how long the little spider had been sealed out of its home in the handle of the looking glass. He knew it had to have been a while. It was glad to be back in the handle, but Vanx could feel the Goss's irritation over having bitten someone that wasn't fully human, too. He was just as irritated as the spider about it.

According to Zythian lore, the bite of the Goss would keep a man tied to the thing for his lifetime. Vanx was no mere man, though. He was half-Zythian, a fact he'd heard the full-blooded Zythians mumbling about earlier. It was strange to hear some of them whispering back in awe of the reputation he'd gained fighting the Paragon, not fear or racial hatred. This made him smile. Now only some of the Zythians despised him for being part human.

It was a start.

He wasn't sure if the Goss would willingly tie itself to a Zythian, or a half-Zythian, for how long would such a being live? Even Vanx had no idea, for no mixed blooded human-Zythian child had ever survived birth until him.

The idea that the Goddess had sent him into this relieved his worry a little. The Zythians were all sharing his cabin, so he decided to go to the galley, where he had a hammock. The strange box was in the satchel there and he wondered if the Goss had spun another web yet, for there was more Vanx wanted to see. He had to know if the book would tell him where the rest of the gem seeds were, for as soon as they fixed what he'd bungled, they would have to continue what they'd started.

Vanx lit a lantern, trying not to wake Gallarael, Moonsy, or Chelda, who was snoring softly in a rhythm that followed the slow rising and falling of the *Adventurer* as it carved through the waves.

"Kalzafranta Murr," Vanx said, and the lid to the box popped open.

He was disappointed to see that the spider hadn't spun a web yet, but he did feel the sickness slide over him again, if only long enough for him to understand that it was the forest he was feeling. All of the forests.

The feeling left him as fast as it came and the lid to the looking glass case slapped shut, causing Chelda to jump out of her bedroll and hit her head on a beam.

The whole room came alive then as Poops entered and started barking at Chelda's curses.

Vanx couldn't get them to go back to sleep, which was just as well. He was feeling guilty in a way he'd never felt before. Not only had he gotten a handful of his companions killed, a whole forest was wailing in agony because of him. And the Heart Tree, well, the Heart Tree's pain made the rest of the forest's agony seem like little more than agitation.

Chapter Thirty-One

> Old Master Wiggins,
> was dancing at the fair.
> He did a flip, but then he slipped,
> upon his homemade hair.
> – A Parydon street ditty

They made it to the Invisible Island in the early morning, and Vanx knew the only reason they could see it was because he possessed the original map the crazy wizard had given him. Without it, they would have had to rely on the *Adventurer*. His magical ship would have found it, though. It had before.

Two of the Zythians had been to Harthgar and knew the globe, and the trade routes, well enough to know the land mass before them shouldn't be there, but it was. Ronzon anchored the ship where they usually did, for the longboat was already ashore, and that landing afforded them the quickest route to the tormented Heart Tree. Vanx decided that, while Moonsy and the Zythians went about relocating it, he would get Gallarael, Chelda, and the two Zythians least proficient in arcanery, started burning the tree suffocating webs out of the branches. He hoped the Zythians would join them soon, for the island was infested with web wrapped limbs, even wholly covered trees. Clearing the island could take days.

"Cast all the wards you think you'll need, General," Vanx emphasised Moonsy's title to the older Zythian spell casters. "She is thrice your age," Vanx told them. "Don't let her childlike appearance fool you. And she knows right where to go. When you re-sit the tree, the top has to be below the wind line. I'd say, put it right on the shore of the lake opposite the grottoes."

"Yes, sir," Moonsy replied, and Vanx had the thought that she'd never acknowledged him as ranking over her until that moment. He'd heard her respond to Thorn in such a way before, but Thorn *had* ranked over her.

Thorn had died for her.

Moonsy and the older Zyths disappeared from the deck of the ship and reappeared at the ridge top. A moment later, Vanx heard Poops yelping, and Ronzon cursing the land. They were on the beach, near the longboat, and Vanx saw that Poops and Ronzon had appeared in a tangle of leafy vines at the edge of the treeline.

Vanx also saw that the web covered limbs were not just spider webs, they were full of the same red glowing larvae, or maybe worms, he'd seen through the looking glass. Vanx felt the vehement repulsion of the Goss burn through him and he was compelled.

He dropped to his knees, right there, and didn't even mind when Gallarael shifted into her black, hard-skinned, humanoid form right beside him. He spoke the words to open the box and, when it was, he let out a frustrated sigh. After feeling so much emotion coming from the Goss, he'd expected to find a web on the looking glass, but there was none.

Instead, he heard a click, and felt the Goss leap to his hand. He was shocked when he saw it burrow right into his skin. The familiar, sickly feeling came over he and Sir Poopsalot, both.

"Chelda, get them started burning webs." Vanx indicated the dozen or so trees that were fully webbed over. They were scattered sparsely across this side of the ridge. Vanx knew the other side of the hill, the next two valleys really, would be worse. "Even get the small webs." He got the attention of one of the two Zythians left to help Chelda. "Watch out for those red worms. Burn them to ash, but don't set the whole forest aflame doing it."

"Uh, Yusser," he stammered.

"Here." Chelda had already unbundled some torches and was rigging them to the poles they brought.

"Vanx," a hissing voice called. The sound grated up Vanx's spine, for it was Gallarael's mutated call. The sound was chilling, and he remembered a freezing cold night in Cold Port when she found him in an alleyway and scared him so bad he'd nearly shit his pants.

"Come. Look," she beckoned, and he went. They didn't get far, for what she showed him filled his blood with ice. Some of the worms in the webs were growing wings. A few had even ripped their way out of their confinement and were fluttering around like eight-legged dragonflies. These were finger-sized, and had a stinger like a hornet. They seemed to have noticed Vanx and Gal peering at them from a shrub.

The Goss wanted him to get to the section of island they hadn't explored yet, but Vanx didn't know why. He was determined to get the Heart Tree relocated first.

"Burning them isn't going to work Chel," Vanx called before they got too far away. "One of you cast a shielding, one that will keep those away from us." Vanx pointed at one of the bright red things fluttering and zipping about and urged Poops to get as close to the Zythians as they could.

"We have to go keep them off the others so they can relocate the tree." Vanx hated to concede anything, but he saw no other choice here. "Once the tree is moved we can regroup on the *Adventurer*." *We can sail to the shore of the unexplored section of the island.* The Goss thought for him.

Once we save the Heart Tree we will go, Vanx agreed with the little blue thing that had gotten under his skin. As if it concurred, a spell formed on Vanx's lips. It was a spell he'd learned from the Hoar Witch's books, but it wasn't he who dug it out of the back of his mind and caused him to cast it.

His hand pointed up at a web, and a jag of wicked lightning sizzled across the span of air between them. The web burst into flame, and several red worms fell to the ground. Chelda squashed them with her boot as she started the charge up the hill.

The Zythian's shielding was effective, for the frightening looking, elongated, flying spiders couldn't pass the dome shaped field of energy that had surrounded them. There was no telling what sort of venom those stingers would inject, and Vanx didn't want to find out. Poops had an instinctual urge to avoid the things, too. It could be webbing, or pure poison. It was all beyond Vanx's comprehension.

Vanx was glad to find that Moonsy and the Zythians were protected from the score or so of the bugs that buzzed around. Vanx saw that more of the strange things were taking flight every moment. He watched as one of the nasty red things was scorched to sizzling pop when it contacted the elf's shielding.

When they contacted the shield around he, Poops, Chelda and the others, they only bounced off.

Gallarael wasn't inside the protection, Vanx saw, and panic got a hold of him.

"Gallarael!" he yelled. "Gal!"

Out of sheer frustration, Vanx blasted the little flying bastards with the spell the Goss put in his mind. He felt the Goss inside him, getting some sort of satisfaction from the deaths of all the red glowing things, but he didn't understand why.

The ground shook violently then. It sounded as if the fabric of the world was being torn apart. Moonsy, the Zythians, and the whole barn-sized trunk of the jacaranda tree, disappeared from in front of him, and Poops nearly tumbled into the hole that was left behind.

Chapter Thirty-Two

As we sail across his sea,
we honor Nepton's rule.
For if you cross old Nepton,
his waves will swallow you.
– A sailor's song

Moonsy and the Zythians had been circled about the tree when it moved from one place to the next. When it appeared at the lake shore, two of the Zythians ended up waist deep in the lake. One of them started wading to shore immediately. The other stood there a moment, taking in what they had just accomplished.

There was a quick splash, and a long grey-green tail swirled out of the now crimson stained water where the Zythian had just been.

Moonsy started out into the lake to try and look for him, but she stopped cold when another, larger splash resounded. This one sent a wave rolling back. It was powerful enough to wash her off her feet and into Vanx.

Some of the Zythians sent streaks of flame up at the lake dragon. Their magic was hard to see in the bright daylight, and they caused more steam to form than damage. Then one of the older Zyths hit the creature with a magical fist, that caused another roar to fill their skulls, and rattle their teeth.

Behind them, Vanx heard the trees rustling, and Gallarael's feral, feline roar. It was feble in comparison. The lake dragon darted down at another of the Zythians, but Vanx had had enough. He cast the first spell that came to mind and was brought to his knees by the potency the tiny little spider inside him added to his casting.

The whole valley dropped in temperature when Vanx's spell unleashed. It took the water wyrm by total surprise. Not freezing the Zythian that the dragon was about to eat, was a hard thing, but Vanx managed it.

Once the water wyrm's exposed upper section, and part of the lake's surface was frozen, it fell over sideways. Chelda sloshed out and pounded the wyrm's neck and vitals with her heavy war hammer while the Zythian that had cast the fist of energy, helped her with his arcanery.

Around them, the trees exploded with cries of shock and terror. Gallarael came bounding through, only to turn and make a stand amongst them. She'd led a whole mess of the ring tailed tree-coons right into the hornet's nest, so-to speak.

"There is no way to burn out all the webs, Master Malic," one of the Zythians pleaded. Vanx knew he was right, and the Goss wanted them to go immediately to the unexplored section of the island, so Vanx made a decision. He cast his icy blast again, this time all around them, in a great arc.

Several ring-tailed coons and more than a handful of the nasty little red spider-hornets fell from the air. Many a tree's screams went quiet, as the sudden chill sent them into a merciful dormancy.

"Get to the longboat, or go straight to the ship, whichever you can manage." He looked to make sure Gallarael heard him.

The way the venom caused huge, pus filled blisters to swell up on the tree-coons that were bitten, Vanx knew that they were injecting the same wicked stuff that had almost killed Zeezle, or something just as terrible. This part of the island was now little more than a swarm of angry flying spider-hornets and web wrapped trees.

Once he, Poops, Ronzon, and Gallarael, ran to the longboat and Chelda was rowing them toward the ship, Vanx felt the Goss relax. It wanted back in its handle. Just to be rid of the sickly feeling it caused in him, Vanx would have gladly obliged it, but the Goss, as relieved as it was, was already directing Vanx where it wanted them to go.

The *Adventurer* responded as soon as Ronzon cranked the anchor chain in. Moonsy and the Zythians had teleported to the deck, and had the boarding nets and block and tackle ready to bring up the others and secure the longboat.

"Leave the boat on a tether," Vanx told them all. "It is time to see what the last part of this place holds. I'd wager there are plenty of those damn spider things in the trees where we are going, so ward yourselves, and each other, well."

They didn't have to sail long. By the time Moonsy took the Glaive of Gladiolus around, and offered its healing power to them all, the ship was coasting to a stop around the southern tip of the island.

Vanx looked at the map and sipped deeply from a flask of watered brandy. He didn't want to be inebriated, but he thought he might need the extra courage the stuff might afford him for there was no telling where the Goss wanted him to go.

In his head, he saw himself standing before something huge and powerful, and the fact that he couldn't tell what it was only served to make the vision that much more intimidating.

This section of the island was the smallest, at least as far as the magical barriers were concerned. In fact, this section was tiny compared to the other two. Still, it was large enough to sustain larger creatures. Some unexpectedly dangerous beast could be waiting as the Goss led he and his friends to it. And even from the sea they could see that there were plenty of the familiar looking webbings choking the trees in this area.

"Go secure us a landing and we will come when it is clear," Moonsy said, handing him back the ancient elven sword.

"We will." Vanx looked down and grasped her by the shoulders. "Take Poops below. He isn't coming this time."

The dog gave protest, both with barks of irritation and in Vanx's mind, but Vanx ignored him.

As soon as Moonsy had the dog below deck, Vanx, Gallarael, and Master Ruuk, were in the longboat and Chelda rowed it to the shore.

Chapter Thirty-Three

> Her kiss was like a candle flame,
> and it burned when she touched him.
> When two days passed and it still burned,
> he knew she'd gave him something.
> – A sailor's song

The Zythians who teleported to the island were afraid. They'd lost one of their companions to the lake dragon and were not all that seasoned, save for the one who volunteered to go into the island's interior with Vanx, Ruuk, Chelda, and Gal. His name was Master Practon. Moonsy was to stay with the other Zythians and keep burning the webs out of the trees along the shore. More importantly, she was to keep the *Adventurer* in sight, and their landing area secure, in case they all had to flee in a hurry.

Vanx figured every little bit of web burning would help. The Goss seemed to agree, but was causing Vanx's blood to itch. There was something urgent going on, and since Vanx now understood he couldn't take his time about finding and relocating the gem-seeds anymore, he thought the whole world might be coming undone as they stood there.

The Goss sent a wave of less nauseating agreement washing through him, but it didn't make Vanx feel any better to know he was right. The Goss was urging him, though, so he followed, knowing that his friends were following because they trusted him and thought he knew what he was doing. He wished he did, but he didn't have any idea what fate awaited them.

Master Ruuk's shielding not only sizzled any of the hornet spiders to a cinder when they came in contact with the field, but it gave off a low vibrating hum, which deterred the winged bastards from getting too close in the first place.

They wound their way up the mountainous hill, and it wasn't long before Vanx could hear, and then see, a great waterfall tumbling down the massive upthrust of rock that separated this area from the rest of the island.

"The mountain itself is a divider," Ruuk observed. "The barriers you showed me on that map run down the ridgelines, I'd guess."

They did, but here was this healthy waterfall, right in the middle. For a moment, something came to Vanx. The idea that the boundaries had been formed more to protect this grand valley with an open view of the sea than for any other purpose made sense, but they all converged on the lazing stone, on the other side of the mountain, not here.

The Goss led him through a thorny thicket, and tried to get them in a shrub field. They skirted that, and walked right onto a flat walking path that led under, and behind, the waterfall's heaviest flow.

There were several columns, all in a perfect row, and they had carvings on them but Vanx couldn't focus on the detail. Master Practon offered to stay at the entry alcove they found. The others started up the stairs leading in.

"Keep this exit clear," Master Ruuk told the other Zythian.

"If you hear us leaving another way, you might want to mark your way back to the ship in a hurry," Chelda said. "The last time we went in a place like this, we ended up a dozen miles away from where we started."

"'Tis true," Vanx agreed. "By the Goddess, I miss that dog's senses when he isn't here," Vanx grumbled more to himself than any of them.

Usually he could draw upon Poops's keener hearing and sense of smell. His own senses had sharpened, and the sickly feeling of the sea compromising his magic had gone away once he bonded with the pooch, though. He loved Sir

Poopsalot immensely. He loved Gallarael, too, even if her current bipedal, black, hard-skinned form wasn't appealing. He loved Chelda and even Master Ruuk, and he did his best to convey these emotions to the Goss. He wasn't sure if the strange spider understood, or not, and now, as they came upon a row of man high symbols, carved into panels on the wall of the cavern the hall lead them into, he knew it was time to either flee or trust the Goss.

The dank chamber was only illuminated because of Master Ruuk's light spell. Chelda was running her hands in the channel of a helmeted man's skull. She was in awe of the simple, yet perfectly clear chiseling of the warrior, but it looked like she was picking the depicted man's nose.

"Just—," he stammered. "Just wait here."

Vanx then went to the center symbol. It was a crude rendering of a man with a spider in his belly. The spider was exactly like the spider on the handle of the looking glass, and what happened next surprised everyone, except for Vanx.

Vanx stood with his back to the symbol. The panel made a grating sound as it flipped, in half a heartbeat, leaving Vanx's friends looking at whatever was carved on the back of the stone slab.

Vanx's cool left him when he saw several hundred sets of eyes looking back at him. He cast a light spell into existence. It was the equivalent of a healthy candle, and its illumination revealed a hundred or more blue streaked spiders, of all shapes and sizes.

Behind him, he could hear Chelda banging on the panel with her war hammer. He almost laughed despite the utter fear that gripped him.

Having experienced Sissy in the Hoar Witch's dungeon, he knew what these arachnoids could do to him, if they chose. The fact they hadn't yet was his only solace.

Compelled forward by the Goss inside him, he moved slowly down the spider-lined corridor, marveling at the differences of them. They were all individually marked with a unique sky blue pattern on their abdomen, but some were long and aggressive looking, while others seemed more reclusive and shy. His heart started to calm until he found he'd been ushered into a larger cavern. He felt the Goss leave him then, and a huge, blue glowing spider dropped from above. It had several sets of eyes, and fangs dripping hot lime colored stuff that Vanx figured would pulp his insides while he hung cocooned somewhere.

Thinking clearly now that the spider's taint no longer had him feeling ill, he cast a protection, and then drew his sword. He didn't square off with the thing or make any other aggressive move. He just drew his sword and stood there.

The spider darted in though and, after Vanx leapt out of its way, it started circling, making its intention to fight him very clear.

Chapter Thirty-Four

On an old barrel keg,
in the shade I sat.
With my pint of watered ale,
and that skinny old cat.
– Parydon Cobbles

Vanx wasn't sure if he should kill the thing or not, but he wasn't about to let it get him so easily.

He tried relying on magic, not his blade, and found that so many spells came to mind that he couldn't choose one.

The spider was chest high to him, and as big as a horse in the middle. Apparently, the numerous other arachnids were being held at bay, by fear or force, Vanx couldn't guess. All he knew was he was leaping in a somersault through appendages lined with grasping little spikes, past green venom dripping fangs, only to land on the spider's middle section.

From there, Vanx cast the most powerful light spell he could muster.

Moonsy would be proud. He laughed at himself. *And Chelda's tongue would finally be stilled if they could see.*

This orb was stark and harsh and caused a multitude of the larger spider's chums to scoot back and even recede from the chamber.

"Do you want to die?" Vanx yelled as he back flipped off the thing before it could shake him free.

Can you kill me? A voice resounded in his head. It was deep and ancient and as full of curiosity as it was anger.

The spider spun then and darted in far faster than Vanx was ready for. It rose up, and used its front legs to coral him, and then it brought its fangs down hard.

Vanx's magical protection scalded the spider's maw, and maybe broke one of its teeth.

"Can you kill me is the question?" Vanx returned.

The spider disappeared from in front of him then, and Vanx's light spell vanished. Vanx fell to his knees and crumpled into a heap on the filthy uneven floor.

Yes I can, came the voice. The Goss was inside him again. He could feel that it was what was speaking to him. It was what he'd just faced, what had just stolen his mind and will from him. It had left him on the floor, unable to escape the score of spiders that were, even now, closing in to devour him.

Just as he started to feel the hairy feelers touching him, another grating sound filled his ears. Up from the floor, a round pedestal rose. Sitting on it was a sapphire gem-seed. It's glow, and the power radiating from it, caused the spiders around him to recede.

There is no time to waste, the voice warned. *We must quicken the seed before the moon turns or all of us will perish.*

"Where do we smash it?" Vanx asked, feeling stupid for talking to himself in an eerie blue glowing chamber.

You must use the gossamer lens, the voice responded. And Vanx wasn't sure that the little spider wouldn't just recluse into the handle of the looking glass and stay there, but even if it did, he would be rid of the sickly feeling.

It was worth a try.

Just then, Chelda finally cracked the stone panel. Vanx grabbed the gem-seed and ran, more by memory than by sight, toward the sound. Her next blow shattered the rock and filled the halls and chamber, now behind him, with bright daylight.

Vanx heard Chelda screaming and Gallarael cursing, when all the blue tinted spiders swarmed over them and raced into the forest.

141

"Kill them." Chelda batted at her hair after they were all gone. "Kill them Vanx, get them off me."

"Look." Gallarael's voice shifted from slithery and felinic, to her human tone, as her body shifted, too.

Vanx had to shake a chill from his spine, but he was no less transfixed by what she was indicating.

The blue spiders were making great net-like webs between the trees. When the red glowing hornets would get caught in the webs, the smaller blue arachnids would speed in and cocoon them.

Dead limbs fell to the ground. After they crashed, the larvae in the suffocating webs were spun into cocoons by spiders controlled by the Goss.

This sensation carried right over the ridge. A few huge white marked tarantula-like spiders emerged from somewhere and, after toppling the trees that had been killed by the spider webs, they crossed right past the boundary as if it was no longer there.

It was then that Vanx heard the strange colored dragon's roar.

He didn't see it, but he had the feeling he would be back here. Not anytime soon he hoped, for through the forests, a war of spiders was raging. The blue marked ones went after the red marked ones, and the white marked arachnids that shared the section of the island the dragon used, started killing all of the others, no matter their color.

"To the ship," he ordered. "We have what we need, and the book should tell us where to go."

With that, they hustled right past Master Practon, and then made their way back to the shore. A few moments later, they were all back on the *Adventurer*.

The ship started sailing without a heading, just to avoid the curiosity of the angry dragon now circling over the spider infested island.

"I hope they all kill each other!" Chelda said while stripping on the deck. Vanx didn't wait to see how that turned out. Instead, he hurried to his cabin and opened the wooden box, allowing the Goss back into the handle of the looking glass.

When he shut the lid and opened the Tome of Arbor, he knew, without a doubt, the spider was weaving him a gossamer lens. The ship sensed this, too, and was ready to know their destination.

It was just bad luck that all the extra Zythians were still aboard. There was no time to drop them off unless their destination turned out to be the Isle of Zyth, but that would be up to the Goss.

The End of Book Nine - The Tome of Arbor

Please enjoy the first three chapters of:

The Legend of Vanx Malic Book 10
A Gossamer Lens

Copyright 2016 Michael Robb Mathias Jr.

All Rights Reserved

Chapter One

At the first sign of disease, certain shoots and runners should be nipped. Never give a blight enough time to infect the sap, for this could be detrimental.

- The Tome of Arbor

Vanx Malic looked at the little blue spider still spinning its web inside the box. It was doing so inside the open ring of the golden looking glass he'd found. The Goss, as the tiny blue marked, arachnoid was called, was no less strange than the box or the looking glass. The magic of the web it was spinning was far stranger than any of it. Or maybe it was the looking glass that added the magic. Vanx hadn't figured it out yet.

Either way, by looking through a lens formed of the spider's silk, he'd seen the pages of the

Tome of Arbor come to life. This time he was hoping to have a longer experience and a chance to read what was written about each tree.

Of course, he would do those things after he learned where the sapphire gem-seed in his satchel needed to grow and made sure they were on the fastest route there. They had very little time to place it and, if they failed, they would all die, so getting that part done was paramount.

His ship, the Adventurer, had taken them out into the open sea, where they were, more-or-less, sailing in circles, waiting to learn where they needed to go. The sea was calm but the swells were large and caused the ship to lean one way or the other as it went.

The island they'd just left could still be seen on the horizon. The consensus was that no one on board wanted to go back there right now. Millions of spiders, some marked with red glowing starbursts, some marked with bright blue stripes, or splotches, as the Goss was, were all battling in the forests. A score of albinic, ship-sized tarantulas that looked to have not seen the light of day for the entirety of their lives, had joined the fray as they were leaving. Vanx figured the three boundary walls were down, for the pale spiders had come from the second area they'd visited. The area where the dragon had shown itself.

There were giant crabs, birds big enough to snatch an elf from the ground, and packs of savage bear-sized, ring-tailed, tree-coons, too. Those were probably trying to survive the spiders this very moment, but there was also that dragon. The wyrm was coral blue, or maybe light-turquoise, Vanx hadn't been able to study the qualities of tone, because he'd been trying to keep from getting eaten, as Moonsy's friend Anitha had. The wyrm had captured Vanx's attention, though, in a way nothing had in a while. He'd shared time with mighty Pyra, had ridden her back, and battled powerful evil with her.

It was a glorious feeling.

Losing so much could crush a person. Vanx wouldn't let that happen to himself. There was a hole in his heart, and there always would be, but he would not fall into despair over losing her.

Pyra was gone now, but Vanx longed to ride a dragon again. Zeezle was trying to make contact with another wyrm, where they'd rooted the elmwood Heart Tree. Zeezle probably felt the same sort of emptiness over Kelse, the great green dragon's death, as Vanx was feeling. Vanx might be able to do the same with the wyrm on this island, too.

It wasn't as if Vanx had a choice, though. The world was off balance, and the abnormal size of the swells they were riding seemed like proof. Anxiously, he peeked under the lid of the looking glass's wooden case, and saw that the Goss was still busy spinning its web. It paused, and Vanx wasn't sure, but he thought it might have looked back at him and smirked.

He'd figured out that it was the Goss he'd faced in that cavern back on what he would forever recall as Spider Island. Whether the Goss was really that big, or really that small, was the question. It had only fought him long enough to see if he had mettle. It had been testing him. And now, as Vanx thought more about it, he figured the tiny Goss had needed the power of something in that cavern to become so large and intimidating. It was tiny, and no matter how much Vanx didn't like it, the spider was somehow bound to him. Vanx would end that, one way or another, when this was done. Since he was only half human, and therefore not fully controllable, the Goss agreed with the sentiment.

"Where are we going?" Chelda asked from the doorway to his cabin. She was naked, having stripped on deck to make sure she had no spiders in her clothes, and due to her gargan size, she had to stoop over, causing her heavy breasts to pendulum about. She asked him a serious question, but his eyeballs followed her tits until Gallarael's wooden cup bounced off his head.

"Please put some clothes on." Vanx rubbed at the knot.

"Bah," Chelda scoffed.

"The Goss hasn't shown me yet." Vanx glared at Gallarael. "Now both of you, leave me alone until this is done."

"There are seven extra people aboard, Vanx," Chelda growled.

"Six," Vanx corrected, reminding her that one of their group had been eaten by the lake dragon before Vanx froze it. She grunted and made her way to the galley, where they were all sleeping, and all their gear had been re-stowed.

Master Ruuk and his group of Zythians were still on board and, as guests, they were using Vanx's Captain's Cabin and Chelda's forecastle bunk room at night. But according to the Goss, there were only days left before the moon would turn and the world would wobble off its course through the ether and end them all, so the Zythians were along for the ride whether they wanted to be or not.

Unless the Goss sent them to Zyth.

Vanx paced across the floor to shut the door, but Master Ruuk shouldered his way in, and Gallarael came with him.

"They would get out from under foot, if you'd let them come down," Ruuk said.

"I want privacy for this, good Master," Vanx politely stern-talked his elder. Ruuk just nodded in silent agreement and slid into the booth, opposite where Vanx had been sitting. Gallarael slid in beside the older Zythian, allowing Vanx all the room of the other bench seat.

This time, when Vanx opened the lid to the looking glass case, the web was complete. He made an audible gasp when he picked it up by the handle. Magic went tingling through his hand and up his arm, before spreading through his whole person, like a fever chill.

Somewhere above deck, Poops let out a howl of pleasure as the dog felt the same sensation through he and Vanx's familial link.

The webbing was fragile and bowed with its resistance to the air. When the strands were stretched, they crackled a sizzling electric blue color, like winter lightning or a lampfish's bright glowers.

Vanx was compelled to turn the pages of the Tome of Arbor with his free hand. He let the magic direct him with as little resistance as he could manage.

With frantic, unnatural speed, he thumbed through a quarter of the book, only to stop and start going back slowly. Then he was there.

On the page was a map. It showed part of Zyth and Dragon Isle. It even had Parydon Isle, and the Sea Spire, but the spire looked like a crumbled hill, not a sharp black needle. It was marked with—

"Look through the lens, fool." Master Ruuk shook his head.

Vanx did so, and he saw the last thing he wanted to see.

In the mountains, deep into the continent the Parydonians had laid claim to, there was a strange tree sprouting and growing on the page, as if it were formed of some magic flow of spilled blue ink.

Vanx pointed to the place, knowing that the shapes of the land masses had been clear even before he'd looked through the lens.

"That's the farkin' crags," Gallarael cursed, which only happened when something was truly worth cursing over. "Far beyond the boundaries of my brother's kingdom. The giants hold reign there, and the ogres are as thick as flies."

"Great," Master Rukk said. "The Zythians up on deck are nearly petrified with fear, as it is."

"Shhh," Vanx shushed them as he looked deeper into the gossamer lens. He understood that at best, with all their combined magic, they might take three to four days to get the ship to Dyntalla, and from there the location was easily a five or six day trek, unless they left the Zythians behind.

If Moonsy rode Sir Poopsalot, he and Chelda could keep up with them, well enough, and trim a day and a half. Gallarael could easily stay ahead and scout the way.

If they landed on the little beach Vanx knew was between the sea and the Wildwood, they could save another half day.

In the lens, he saw the details of the area the Goss intended him to see. There was a pond formed by a wide flowing stream. It sat in the bottom of a deep valley. A valley that sat too far into the treacherous mountains for his comfort, but there it was, surrounded by strange white bloomed trees with what looked like upward pointing pinecones, only made of thin petals, not hard fibers.

Vanx tried to turn the page of the book to find the type of tree he'd seen growing blue, but the web burned away. The acrid smell that filled his cabin forced him to open the hatch and let fresh air in just to stop coughing.

After a moment, when the air had cleared, Vanx put the looking glass back in its case and closed it. He put the case, and the Tome of Arbor, in his satchel and urged Gallarael out of the cabin, toward the galley.

"Tell the Zythians they can come down now." Vanx grinned through his concern. "After you drop us on the coast, Ronzon and the Adventurer will take you all to Flotsam."

"What if I want to go with you?"

"I won't stop you, but you'll have to keep up." Vanx shrugged. "The moon will turn far too soon, and the world will come apart before we can even make it to the location the Goss showed me, as it is. There will be no dallying."

Chapter 2

After discussing it all over that night's supper, it turned out that Master Rukk wasn't the only Zythian who wanted to go with them. Another, who was a little older than Vanx, and had some experience, did too. Vanx was glad it was Master Practon. He'd gone onto the spider infested island with them, and Vanx knew he wouldn't panic, if things got tricky.

Gallarael was against Vanx's idea of landing in the Wildwood instead of Dyntalla. Vanx couldn't blame her. She'd entered that place a fairly innocent princess and ended up whatever she was now, a changeling, a shapeshifter, whatever. But in the end, she was agreeable to the plan, if that is what you could call it.

Gallarael had a valid argument, saying they could get horses and mountaineering supplies in Dyntalla, just on her name. But Vanx reminded her the truth of it. They would be hassled and questioned and slowed, just by having to explain themselves. She was the King's sister, and her presence there, or anywhere in the human kingdom, for that matter, would cause an uproar.

If they were hassled in the Wildwood, they could just use Moonsy and Ruuk's protective spells, or diplomacy, and keep going. The kobles, and the lesser ogres they might come across, would want no part of this group, Vanx figured. And if they were challenged, Chelda could smash their skulls flat with her war hammer.

The river that fed all of that vegetation would be flowing slow, for autumn was upon them. The wash-out along the river bed would make a perfect trail for them to follow inland. They didn't have time to worry about cold weather gear, for the world would come apart if they failed. The climbing equipment Gallarael spoke of could be rigged out of rope, hinge pins, and the smaller block and tackle they had on the ship. It would be crude, but it would keep them together if they needed it to.

Vanx thought he had everything covered.

"I suggest that Chelda be in charge of rigging the personal lanyards." Vanx gave Gallarael a funny look. Chelda was on deck, probably telling Ronzon and the younger Zythians some wild tale. "She has the most climbing experience."

"I can out climb all of you," Gallarael fired back.

"But we can't grow claws," Vanx squeezed her shoulder and fought back the revulsion thoughts of her changing caused to roil through his gut. "I meant Chelda knows best how to make use of what we have, for those of us who can't scale cliff faces and folded stairs. She grew up climbing mountains."

"What about Poops?" Gallarael asked then.

Vanx pondered it a minute, even though he knew the dog would go. He didn't like going anywhere without his familiar, but the mountains would be a challenge for the pooch.

"I think Moonsy will ride and protect him fiercely." Vanx finally said. "Just like Thorn did."

"Yup," Gallarael said the single word mocking Vanx's use of it. This caused them both to laugh, but Vanx noticed Master Ruuk wasn't even smiling.

Vanx grew serious. "Did you know him well?" Vanx asked cautiously. "The Zythian who was—well—who was taken by the lake wyrm?"

"Nah, nah." Ruuk waved a hand to show he wasn't dwelling on that. "He was a good person, but I hardly knew him. I was just wondering about the giants." Ruuk unrolled one of the maps Vanx often used because it showed all of the ports in the area.

They were still in the Galley, it being their turn to clean up after the evening meal. Moonsy alertly wiped the central table clean so the old Zythian could use it as a map table. "This far into the mountains," he pointed to roughly where Vanx had indicated they needed to go. His finger was at the farthest edge of their map. Their destination, Vanx knew, wasn't even on the parchment, "there are savage tribes of barbaric giants, and they are constantly warring over territory." He studied the map a little closer. "Could you call Master Practon down before you retire? I may have a way to save us some more time, but I would confer with him first."

"I'll tell him," Gallarael said, brushing by Vanx, intentionally rubbing his crotch with her firm arse. "After I tell Chelda what you want her to do, Master Vanx."

Why she continually had to arouse him was a concern. The constant shifting from repulsion to attraction was making his head swim and starting to take its toll on his patience. This was no time for him to be distracted but, then again, they couldn't really do anything besides lay around until they made shore.

With that thought, Vanx went down into the bulkhead to look for something to use to make a lifting harness for Poops, in case they had to haul him up a mountainside or something. He thought there was a set of leather straps on a pallet that had been brought over from the Ada Rosamond, and he was right. There were some good steel rings, and lacing, too. Then he saw the lamp and used a spell to light it and give him a little more light. That was when he saw what the stuff was really there for.

Chelda was making a pair of saddles for the horses she'd left back on Dragon Isle. Vanx was surprised, but not shocked. He knew she was creative, for she'd carved out the detail and painted the Adventurer's Mystica masthead. The ship was very proud of it, too. She was making two saddles, it turned out. He only hoped she would understand the need here.

Chapter 3

"If we are all going to die, if we don't get this done, I'll use any of it," Chelda said. She'd come down and was crawling toward Vanx on her hands and knees. Vanx saw that, due to her gargan size, she'd had to crawl amongst the barrels and sit cross-legged to do her crafting. "I've formed mine and Moonsy's cantle and pommels already. The rest is just fitting it all together. We can use it, but how'd you know?"

"I didn't," Vanx was stooped over and now understood what Chelda had to go through when moving about in the normal sized interior of the ship. "I just remembered loading some leather strapping and came to see if I was right."

"Don't tell Moonsy," Chelda's tone grew firm. "Her saddle is a surprise."

"Rig it to fit Poops, not a horse, Chelda." He grinned at their fortune. "She'll need to ride Poops to keep up with us once we get going." As he turned, he bumped his head on a beam, and heard whoever was above him shuffle their feet, startled.

"Yah. I can do that." Chelda laughed at his folly. "That, and make some good lanyards. If you see Moonsy, send her down. There is no sense in holding the surprise back now, and she can get around down here way better than I can."

"I will." Vanx excused himself, not sure why he felt embarrassed over finding Chelda's private place. His private place was atop the mast pole, not in the crow's nest, but actually atop the pole, with his legs wrapped in the rigging to hold him in place when the ship swayed back and forth.

There, he could sink into Poops sensory perception and take in the world as no one else could. It was the closest thing to riding a dragon's back he could manage, and he relished it, even though it didn't quite compare.

After sending Moonsy down to help Chelda, and telling Gallarael what supplies to put in he and Chelda's backpacks, he climbed the thick, tar saturated mast and got situated.

He thought about how it would be hacking a way through the Wildwood, opposite the protected trade route that had been established. They could cause a war if they were thought to be Parydonians.

Vanx wasn't worried about that too much, though. Gallarael was the only human among them, and she would probably be in one of her shifted forms most of the time. Mistaking them for poachers or lost travelers was not going to happen. They had a seven and a half foot tall gargan woman with them and an elf who would be riding his dog familiar. Anything with any sense would flee.

*

Two days passed, and the dragon they'd left behind kept stealing Vanx's thoughts. The light sea colored wyrm was just the right size to carry him. He'd climbed up high to get away from everyone for a while. It was late evening, and the cool autumn sky was filled with stars. He felt the mast pole shiver when one of the Zythians directed a wind spell at the sails. They been doing this in rotation since they'd learned the route they were taking.

The Zythians, who were not going, were pleased to learn they would have passage back to Zyth. Their enthusiasm showed in their spell casting, for the Adventurer was gliding across the waves at a sharp rushing clip.

In fact, with Poops's keen nostrils, Vanx could already smell fire smoke coming from the land. They would see the shore before the sun came up, he was sure.

Vanx made his way down to the deck. He lit and hung a lantern and used a shovel to scoop Poops shit out of the rectangular turf box he'd built for the dog. Then he used a sprinkler can to water the grass.

Master Practon had shown him a spell that would help keep the grass nutrified, but he had to find the time to dig up some ground worms to make it all self-sustaining with the arcanery.

He heard Ronzon swear and went up to the open wheel house to see what was amiss. He saw the orange flicker before he even had the long tube Ronzon handed him in his grasp. When he found it in the glass, he was stupefied.

"No way." He shook his head in wonder.

"Are them ogres?" Ronzon asked, the fear in his voice as clear as his words.

"Yes they are, my friend." Vanx laughed and gave the man a reassuring squeeze on the shoulder. "They are compelled to follow the blood stone, but it is in Pyra's hoa—" Vanx stopped himself. "It is somewhere else."

Ronzon was a mere human, and no matter how hard he tried, if he knew there was a dragon's hoard on the island they'd left Zeezle on, the man would be tempted by greed. For his own good, Vanx left that part out.

Ronzon gulped audibly.

Vanx watched through the long glass, as one of the score of enraged ogres left the bonfire and charged into the sea. It waded until it had to swim. Then, when it was just beyond the roll of the surf, something snatched it from below.

"How are we going to land there?" Ronzon asked. "I counted three dozen of them."

"Three dozen?" Vanx looked at him and smiled. "I'll wager my ten coins to your one Chelda Flar can clear that fire by herself."

"Ten to one?" Ronzon's fear was suddenly gone. "I think I'll have to put three pieces of gold on that one, sir." The seaman showed his three coins, but kept his head down. "Though, I'd hate to see Lady Chelda fall, just to make my fortune."

"You just lost three pieces of gold, Ronzy." Chelda stepped up between them. She was holding one of the other tubes. Vanx came up to her chin, but Ronzon's head was right at breast level.

"Well, hell," the seaman said. "Can I get off the bet for one, Captain?"

"You can," Chelda answered for Vanx. "And if you ask me, too, I'll go kill them all, Vanx, but I have a better idea, and one coin in the hand is better than three in the wind."

"Can't argue that one," Vanx winked as he took Ronzon's coin, and put a bite on it to make sure it was soft. "Debt paid," he said when he found it was. Then he turned to Chelda.

"Now tell me about this plan."

The End
(of the book ten sample)

Other titles by M. R. Mathias

The Legend of Vanx Malic
Book One – Through the Wildwood
Book Two – Dragon Isle
Book Three – Saint Elm's Deep
Book Four – That Frigid Fargin' Witch
Book Five – Trigon Daze
Book Six – Paragon Dracus
Book Seven – The Far Side of Creation
Book Eight – The Long Journey Home
Book Nine – The Tome of Arbor
Book ten – A Gossamer Lens

The Saga of the Dragoneers
The First Dragoneer – Free for Kindle
The Royal Dragoneers – Nominated, Locus Poll 2011
Cold Hearted Son of a Witch
The Confliction
The Emerald Rider
Rise of the Dragon King
Blood and Royalty – Winner. 2015 Readers Favorite Award,
and 2015 Kindle Book Award Semifinalist

The Wardstone Trilogy
Book One - The Sword and the Dragon
Book Two - Kings, Queens, Heroes, & Fools
Book Three - The Wizard & the Warlord

Short Stories:

Crimzon & Clover I - Orphaned Dragon, Lucky Girl
Crimzon & Clover II - The Tricky Wizard
Crimzon & Clover III - The Grog
Crimzon & Clover IV - The Wrath of Crimzon
Crimzon & Clover V - Killer of Giants
Crimzon & Clover VI – One Bad Bitch
Crimzon &Clover VII – The Fortune's Fortune

Master Zarvin's Action and Adventure Series #1
Dingo the Dragon Slayer
Master Zarvin's Action and Adventure Series #2
Oonzil the oathbreaker
Master Zarvin's Action and Adventure Series #3
The Greatest Quest

To hear about new releases,
sales and giveaways,
follow M. R. Mathias @DahgMahn on
Facebook, Twitter, and Instagram, or visit
www.mrmathias.com

CPSIA information can be obtained
at www.ICGtesting.com
Printed in the USA
BVHW03s1050050718
520875BV00001B/23/P 9 781946 187369